A LC

The worst of it was following Howard out of class and down the hall, watching people react. Some who had seen him earlier said loud, good-natured hi's while nudging whoever they were walking with. Faces wore hidden shock, open shock, careful control, unsuccessful control. And some of them passed him right by because they didn't recognize him at all. And if he said hi, which he was doing as if things were normal, some would turn suddenly and look back and give one of those oh-my-God-is-that-really-you-Howie looks that were the worst of all. No, worse even was an occasional betrayal of malice, a mean little gleam of "and you always thought you were hot stuff, Nevelson."

Bo had absorbed all of this, walking behind him. There was a point where she could have turned, should have, and gone up the stairway and to her locker, thrown in her books, found Weezie, and limped home. But somehow she felt obliged to stay behind him, receiving it all, as if she could attract some of his pain and let him suffer the less. She knew then that she would have to keep doing that if she could. If it happened that he would let her.

Other Bantam Starfire Books you will enjoy

PEOPLE LIKE US by Barbara Cohen
THE PERFECT GUY by Ann Herrick
HOME SWEET HOME by Jeanne Betancourt
LEAVE ME ALONE, MA by Carol Snyder
AMONG FRIENDS by Caroline B. Cooney
THE THINGS I DID FOR LOVE by Ellen Conford
HOLDING ME HERE by Pam Conrad

A Lot Like You

Judith Pinsker

BANTAM BOOKS
NEW YORK · TORONTO · LONDON · SYDNEY · AUCKLAND

RL 6, IL age 10 and up

A LOT LIKE YOU
A Bantam Book
Bantam hardcover edition / February 1988
Bantam paperback edition / May 1989

*The Starfire logo is a registered trademark of Bantam Books,
a division of Bantam Doubleday Dell Publishing Group, Inc.
Registered in U.S. Patent and Trademark Office and elsewhere.*

*Grateful acknowledgment is made for permission to reprint lyrics from
"Come Saturday Morning," by Dory Previn and Fred Karlin, copyright
© 1969 by Famous Music Corporation.*

Library of Congress Cataloging-in-Publication Data

Pinsker, Judith.
A lot like you.

Summary: An obese fifteen-year-old receives a shock
when she returns to school in the fall and finds that
her formally thin heartthrob has gained a lot of weight
following the death of his mother in an automobile crash.
[1. Obesity—Fiction] I. Title.
PZ7.P6347Lo 1988 [Fic] 87-19534
ISBN 0-553-27852-5

Published simultaneously in the United States and Canada

PRINTED IN THE UNITED STATES OF AMERICA

O   0 9 8 7 6 5 4 3 2 1

for Adam

A Lot Like You

1

*H*omeroom. Bo Barrett sat at her desk chewing at her knuckles. She purposely hadn't brought anything edible. A new leaf, a new semester, a new class— sophomores. Howard Nevelson was a senior now and as a senior member of the student council there was a one-in-four chance it would be his voice that would pour out of the public-address system any minute, after Dr. Jackson led the Pledge of Allegiance.

Ms. Palmer sat up front, same as last year, her hands a little shaky, checking off their names in her roll book and playing with a string of her hair. Wouldn't you think she'd wash it for the first day of school? As a role model, Palmer was the pits.

There was a crackling in the air as the P.A. came on. Bo's stomach jumped. Please let it be . . . let it be, please . . . *Dong.* Ms. Palmer looked up stunned as if the P.A. chime were her alarm clock. She got up slowly with the rest of them. They all placed their hands on their hearts.

The announcing voice wasn't Howard's. Bo's stomach settled down sadly and she was sorry she'd made that dumb resolution. At least she could have brought a box of Raisinets. For years she'd been sitting in classes popping Raisinets and feeling better. Still, Howard was worth the sacrifice, if she could just manage to run into him early. It would set a tone for the whole school year. Oh come on. Well, it would make her day, anyway; make her . . . what, she wondered. I don't know, she thought, feeling a little testy by now. Happy? She shrugged to herself and the bell rang.

But the day didn't go Bo's way. Try as she might, she couldn't run into Howard casually anywhere, though she engineered several long-cuts past his locker and one past his girl-friend, Cyndy's. Finally, embarrassed by her obsession, Bo swore she'd leave straight from her own locker when the bell rang, but when she got to the north door with her friend Weezie, she couldn't quite control herself. "Wait here, would you?"

"Why?" Weezie sounded exasperated, which was her normal tone.

"Weeze, I'm sorry, but I've got to go. I had this bladder trouble all summer."

"You never said anything in your letters." Weezie had been at riding camp. Her family had money.

"What's to write about having to pee all the time?"

Weezie rolled her eyes, something she did a lot. "Look, I don't want to stand here like a nerd. I'll come with you."

Bo lowered her voice. "I don't need help, Louise."

"Okay, I'll wait."

Bo moved quickly down the corridor, up one flight, and past Howard Nevelson's locker for the fourth time that day.

Idiot, she said to herself. He's not here. Got it? Howard David Nevelson was not in school today. So? It didn't have to be a big deal, did it? Maybe he was just delayed getting back from vacation. But fear pulled at her. Maybe his father had taken him out of school . . . Maybe they were moving somewhere . . . Maybe they couldn't stand Parkview any-more—too many memories. God help the team, she thought. You can't just move a star of the basketball team and a member of the student council.

Bo couldn't take the thought of losing Howard. Not that she had him, or ever could. What was it she wanted, any-way, looking for him like this? Just for him to say, "Hi," she supposed. Maybe even, "Hi, Bo," proving that he knew her. Maybe he'd even thank her for the sympathy note. So what would she say then?

She had now walked the entire length of the corridor where Howard's locker was located—2N for 2 North—maybe N for Nevelson. She headed straight for the drinking foun-tain, ducked down to drink, and raised up coolly, keeping a thoughtful distant expression ready, rehearsing, *What? Oh, Howard, hi! How was your summer . . . ?* Brilliant, Barbara, she thought. It's a good thing you didn't see him. How do you think the summer is after your mother dies?

What if he showed up and he didn't speak to her at all? It had been four months. Howard spoke to everybody, though. It was one of the things that made him wonderful. He was totally democratic. So how could he forget her, after three weeks of rehearsal and one stirring performance? Tragedy didn't wipe out your memory. Not at Howard's age, anyway. Of course he'd be back. The place couldn't operate without him. It was as if his smile made everybody move in the hall.

Who's Barbara Barrett? she imagined him saying when he'd gotten her note—those stiff little words that had taken a week and a half to write and still didn't say half what she felt. He'd have looked mystified at first, probably, then, *Oh, yeah, from the show, the fat one.*

•   •   •

"Hi, I guess you're my co-star." She was sitting in the auditorium, fourth row, on the aisle, when he came up to her.

"How'd you know?" It was all she could think of to reply, and then felt idiotic about it.

The briefest hesitation, then: "Tippy Carmichael told me about you."

Told you what? Oh, I can just hear her. *"You'll looove Butter Barrett. She's such an incredible sport . . ."* Why did I accept her charity? Why couldn't she just leave the misfits out of her dumb show? Why did I say I'd do it?

"She tells me you're a terrific sport." He was looking right at her.

"Oh. This whole thing was her idea," Bo said generously.

" 'Special Skits for Special People?' " He waved the Xeroxed pages. "That's what it says here. How are you special?"

She took a breath and grinned. "Isn't it obvious?"

He grinned back. Wonderfully, goldenly, taking her meaning without malice. God bless Tippy Carmichael.

"Want to run through it now?"

Now and forever.

•   •   •

Weezie was still waiting by the north door, shifting her slight weight from one leg to another, when Bo reappeared.

"What did you do, fall in?"

"I'm sorry," Bo said, meaning it. "It hurts a lot, that's all."

"It hurts to go?"

"Yeah, my bladder is like in spasm." It was only half a lie; it had been true two weeks ago. ("No clinical reason that I can find, Mrs. Barrett," the doctor had said, as though Bo weren't there. "Has she been under stress?" "Stress?" Her mother had looked scandalized. "She's only fifteen!")

"Are you taking anything for it?" Weezie asked now.

"They can't do anything."

4

"I'm telling you, modern medicine is really the pits. Your average doctor knows nothing."

"Weezie, your father is a doctor."

"That's what I mean," Weezie said, and shrugged. "You know what I think. I think it's your nerves."

Bo's voice became calm, low-pitched, and extremely reasonable. "It's not my nerves, Louise. It's my bladder."

Louise Schultz knew when she was licked. "Okay, okay," she said. "Let's go. It would be nice to get to Mitch's before midnight."

"I don't think so today. I don't want to eat," Bo said.

"Since when?" Weezie asked and started off. Bo followed her.

2

Mitch's was crowded as usual.

"You and your bladder," Weezie said under her breath as they entered. "We could be stuck way up front now." It was well known, if unspoken, that the further back you sat in Mitch's the more accepted and acceptable you were, though Weezie wouldn't have admitted that was on her mind. "I mean you never get any service . . ." she started to add but was distracted by the entrance of a wild-haired boy wearing a T-shirt that read, Whoever Has the Most Things When He Dies, Wins. He had pushed the door open with his knee and now stood surveying Mitch's Place as though he didn't particularly want to be there. "Who is *that*?" Weezie said. "Or should I say *what*?" she added as the boy walked past them giving Bo what appeared to be a nod of acknowledgment. He took the table closest to the door, and plunked down his books as if he were making a statement.

"David Abraham," Bo said as they moved down the aisle toward a group of classmates. "He's in my writing class. Big brain. Angry type, you know? He actually asked Ms. Albersham if she minded four-letter words in the assignments.''

"What did she say?" Weezie was fascinated.

"She said, 'Not if that's all you've got.' "

"At least he's in touch," Weezie said, glancing backward briefly. But she was smiling, however sourly, as she said it, and Bo had applied the merry look that was her official public face as they reached their friends, who were in a booth midway to the back.

"Hello, group," Bo said. "Would two or three sturdy people like to get up and make room for me? Weeze can sit on a lap." There was a general laugh of appreciation. Nobody moved, but Marve Newton signaled grandly to Mitch, calling out, "Innkeeper . . . One tough chair, please." Something inside Bo lurched, still she grinned, and when the chair arrived and was placed in the aisle she made a small good-natured deal of testing its strength. Everyone was watching, grinning, liking her. "There," she said, as if to dismiss them, "now everybody put your arms up and make a space for Weeze." Minor adjustments were made and Weezie wiggled past Bo into the thin space vacated.

"Thank you, Asthma," Marvin said to Weezie and cozied up to Annette Morisi, who gave him a coy grin and went back to looking at herself in the jukebox. Weezie looked to Bo and rolled her eyes, sending the message: good-grief-are-they-a-pair-this-year-I-can't-stand-it. Bo shrugged slightly, helplessly. Marvin nudged Annette with his shoulder and raised his voice to a falsetto. "Hello-ho-ho," he said. Annette giggled.

"Newton, can it, would you?" Weezie said through her teeth. "He's right back there." She nodded toward a booth all the way in the rear.

"I? He? Me? Whatever do you mean?" Marvin continued in a voice clearly mimicking the president of the student council, Dodson L. White.

"Sh-h-h," Bo hissed and gave Marvin a look.

"Well-well-well, my-my-my, Butterball," Marvin continued undaunted. "Is Doddie a special friend of yours? Is there something you haven't told us?"

"Butter, *is* there?" Darlene Pettit asked wide-eyed.

"No, Dar," Bo said back to her patiently, then looked to Marvin. "I just don't think you have to be mean."

"She's right," Mary Katherine Pomeroy put in, "Doddie White is really nice. . . . No, really," she added in response to Marvin's snort. Tiger Yellen, a short pale boy who had profound respect as well as mild lust for Mary Kay, nodded in support.

"He's decent enough," Tiger said. "The whole thing went out of whack, that's all. Nobody meant it to go that far."

"They asked for it," Weezie said, scowling. "They do it every year, and it's lousy. Nominate some poor schnook they can laugh at when he makes his speech."

"Tradition!" Marvin sang out in the manner of *Fiddler on the Roof* and thumped the table. Annette loved it. "He didn't have to take the bait, did he?"

"Of course he did, nitwit," Weezie said. "He'd've been a coward otherwise."

"But I mean," Annette said, "none of the schnooks ever actually got elected before. Do you believe Dopey L. White is going to be squeaking out the announcements every fourth day all year?"

Bo looked toward the back booth wishing she could see Howard there instead of Dodson L. White, who was cackling his weird little laugh, apparently unaware he was a total misfit. She thought of the election assembly, and Doddie making his speech, the odd squeaky lilt to his voice, his wrists showing in the badly fitting sports coat. "Fellow

8

classmates . . .'' he'd started out seriously. He'd said he was really honored. What he is, is brave, she'd thought. People had poked each other in the ribs. Is this guy for real? When it was all over they'd gone back to their homerooms to vote and Dodson White had been elected president. Bo wanted to believe it was not for the worst reasons.

But the student body could be decent, too. After all, they'd also elected Howard to the council. Not unexpected, but unprecedented, since he wasn't there at the time. He'd never come back to school after his mother's accident, six weeks earlier.

"Butter, where are you?" Annette said suddenly, waving her hand in front of Bo's face. Bo was still staring at the booth farthest back, wishing Howard were there where he belonged, among the In people. "Mitch wants to know," Weezie added, protectively. Bo looked up to find Mitch standing over her shoulder waiting with his order pad.

"A Fresca, I guess," she replied.

"That's *all*?" Marvin said, making a big deal of it. Bo noticed Mary Katherine and Darlene were looking at her oddly, too. Did something show? Did her face have I-miss-Howard written across it? ". . . And a slice of Sicilian," she added quickly to Mitch, who made a note of it. Everybody looked satisfied.

I will not think of Howard. I will not think of Howard, Bo chanted to herself like a mantra, and forced her attention to her assembled friends. She'd known most of them since kindergarten, when Marvin was always made to sit in the hall and Tige brought in samples of bugs for show-and-tell and Annette had a crush on Ritchie Stewart who had moved to Peoria in the second grade. It seemed, too, as if they had always watched her eat and had had something to say about it. She didn't mind so much, really, if they needed her for that. Maybe she needed them for that, too.

Bo made an effort to join the conversation, asking Tiger who he'd pulled for history.

"Palumbo," he replied.

"Lucky dog. You'll spend all your time on the Renaissance," she said.

"How do you know, Butterball?" Marvin asked. Weezie's eyes flashed and she looked to Bo, whose smile simply widened.

"I know a lot. Somebody said so." Bo knew because Howard Nevelson, who'd had Mr. Palumbo for world history, had told her so, on the occasion of one of their four conversations—she clenched her teeth against this train of thought and made herself go on. "MK, what about you?"

Mary Kay looked despondent. "Calisher."

There was a general groan.

"Not a giant intellect, I fear," Bo said and sighed in condolence.

"So what," Marvin said. "At least she won't have to work."

"Some of us like to work," Tiger said. Mary Kay rewarded him with a nice smile.

"Some of us like to cut up turtles and check out their gross insides," Annette said. Tiger, whose real name was Sanford, had achieved misfit fame at Parkview last year by keeping a heart-transplanted turtle alive for forty minutes.

"Whatever turns you on," Marvin said, and gave Annette a little pinch. "At least Calisher is sober," he added. "Speaking of which, will you be joining us in Palmer's second-period free-for-all, Butterball?"

"I'm taking geometry, if that's what you mean," Bo said pleasantly.

"HIC!" Marvin said.

"You are such an infant, Newton," Weezie remarked. "Palmer has a problem."

"Which is not a chronic cough," Marvin snorted. "In

case you thought what was in that little bottle was Robitussin.'' Annette put her hand on his wrist and leaned forward sputtering with laughter.

"Holy sin!" Weezie said suddenly, her eyes on the door. "Is that or is that not Randall with Larry Kirby?" Bo turned her head so quickly that her weight shifted and the chair almost went over. It was indeed Cynthia Randall—Cyndy the gorgeous, the confident, the smart, the for-two-years steady girl of Howard Nevelson—walking casually toward the In-people's booth, hand in hand with Larry Kirby.

"Where's Howie?" Annette whispered, wide-eyed.

"Nowhere, obviously," hissed Weezie, and shot a look to Bo, who was trying to keep her face together.

"Did they break up?" Darlene asked, clearly scandalized.

"I didn't hear that," a voice squeaked. It was Bo.

"News to me."

"I doubt it."

"Then she's a two-timer," Annette said, nodding toward the back. Larry and Cyndy had squeezed into the booth, backs to the fascinated onlookers. His arm could be seen around her shoulder.

"Just goes to show you," Weezie said. "Never trust anybody who spells her name with two Y's."

"She wouldn't do that," Bo said, forcibly controlling her voice.

"Why not?" The question came from Marvin. "Nevelson's been gone all summer."

"But his mother," Bo said, bewildered. "Cyndy wouldn't. Not when . . .''

"Absence is supposed to make the heart grow fonder, isn't it?" Darlene offered.

"Only if you're over fifty," Weezie said.

"Butter, your pizza's getting cold," Mary Kay said, genuinely concerned.

11

"She likes it better that way," Marvin said. "Goes down faster." Bo said nothing and took a bite.

"Marvin," Weezie said sweetly, "kindly stifle yourself."

Marvin didn't, of course. Bo let them trade insults around her and continued to observe the back booth. It appeared to be true. Cyndy Randall was sitting there eating fried onion rings and allowing Larry Kirby to keep his arm around her.

Why is this so weird? she asked herself. People break up all the time. Maybe Howard got tired of Cyndy. Wait . . . he hasn't moved away, has he? Tell me he hasn't. Maybe she got tired of him. How could she? Ever? Just for a moment Bo let herself see him in her head, tall and perfect. The sweetness of his face, the gentleness, the whole sense of him filled her and made her warm and confused. She looked at Cynthia and at Larry Kirby, who couldn't hold a candle to Howie. If Cyndy had broken it off, why? If that girl had hurt him, after what he'd been through this spring . . . Anger welled in her. She took a large bite of pizza and it slid down her throat. She looked over at the booth again. For whatever reason, Cyndy and Larry Kirby were now clearly a pair. And that left Howard . . . where? Single, so to speak? Not that it made any difference. She looked at her own reflection in the jukebox. The ripples in the chrome gave her even more chins.

3

*M*ost of the time Bo was looking for him, Howard Nevelson was sitting on the couch at home, trying to read and trying to get comfortable. He picked up a pillow from one end, stuck it under his knees, and slithered down a little. The book was too high. He removed the pillow and studied it a moment: bargello, in mixed blues with a line here and there of bright yellow. His father always said that his mother's needlework was the only place she ever achieved order.

The house had always been littered with her intentions—stacks of mail impatiently ripped open and set aside, swatches of fabric on which no decision was ever made. The only birthday cards she'd ever sent were belated. The house was neater since she'd been gone. His dad tended to throw things away without looking at them, and Mrs. Flanders, the latest housekeeper, polished a lot, twice a week. But his mother's gentle chaos was missing.

Howard put the pillow behind his head and propped the

book on his stomach. Honors history. Barbara Tuchman on the fourteenth century. It slid off. He balanced it against his knees and started to read again.

After the experience of the horrible 20th century, we have a greater fellow-feeling for a distraught age whose rules were breaking down under the pressure of adverse and violent events. We recognize . . .

Howard's mind wandered. He remembered Palumbo saying how they weren't into sanitation and things back then, how they threw garbage out the window. He saw himself walking down a street in the fourteenth century. Stone walls with little windows. Little tiny windows raining rotten fruit and coffee grounds. Coffee grounds? Suddenly a small red car came careening down the twisted street behind him. He jumped out of the way. The car smashed into the castlelike wall. There was a bang and then a silence.

He started the paragraph over. The phone rang. He righted himself slowly and reached for it.

"So when do we see you, Howie?" It was the Moose, his political science teacher and coach, calling. Former coach. "I need my devil's advocate for Friday discussion."

"I'm supposed to stay off my feet. At least till the tests come back."

The Moose sort of grunted in a way he had that said, I see but was noncommittal. "How does basketball fit in?"

Howard hedged. Moose would know soon enough. "I don't know. Maybe it doesn't."

The Moose hesitated a moment, then said, "Well, let's not borrow trouble." Now he had a false smile in his voice. "You've had enough already." Howard coughed. The Moose went on, "Okay, what I gave you should take care of the week's work. Don't overdo, though. You can always catch up."

"Right," Howard said. "Thanks."

He propped the book up again and looked for his place. *Adverse and violent events . . .*

We recognize with a painful twinge the marks of "a period of anguish when there is no sense of an assured future."

When his father came in at five, Howard was asleep.

4

Weezie had scowled most of the way home from Mitch's. Bo knew she was waiting to be asked what was wrong, but her own energy was flagging. She tried in general to listen to Weezie's frequent tirades. After all, what were friends for? Nobody listened much to Weezie. Her family threw her designer items and fancy lessons like dog biscuits, to keep her quiet. She was muttering now as they walked, since her scowls hadn't roused Bo's interest. "I'm telling you . . . I'm telling you . . ." she said to herself, just loud enough. Bo gave in. She could think about Howie from the corner of Ash Street, where Weezie would turn off.

"Telling me what?"

"Huh?"

"What's the matter?" Bo tried not to sigh.

"Nothing," Weezie said, as usual.

"Come on."

"It's just . . . They really fry me, those creeps."

"Which?"

"Our so-called friends."

"How come?"

"Don't you know? Don't you really know?" Weezie now wore her full irate look, which said clearly the whole world is an outrage and you are dumb not to know it.

"No," Bo said. "I don't know. You're the one who's mad."

"Of course." Weezie was now in her element. "That's always the way. It's you they insult and me who gets mad."

"I don't insult easy."

"God knows." Weezie looked heavenward. "God only knows."

Bo grinned. "Why should I? You handle it for both of us." Weezie, who knew this, too, and sometimes had the grace to laugh over it, didn't laugh this time. As she went into her full complaint, Bo turned an adjustment inside her head: volume to low. She could catch the drift this way; she had many times. Snatches of her best friend's voice reached her: ". . . Marvin-Gardens Newton. The cheapest block on the board. Sure he paid for Annette's coke, but I notice he doesn't contribute to the tax, and if he left a tip it was a nickel. Okay, the business with Annette, who cares, but he was so mean to you. That number with the chair. Butter, where's your pride sometimes?" Bo knew she didn't want an answer. Weezie went on nonstop while Bo had a sudden not unhappy remembrance of the two of them at eleven, clutching books, walking home in the other direction from Eisenhower Elementary. Two junior-high boys had arrived behind them. Cracking voices came over their heads:

"Hey, what happened to the view?"

"I don't know. Total eclipse?" A slightly dark feeling accompanied the memory into Bo's stomach.

"That's not an eclipse. It's a boxcar."

"That's no boxcar. It's a hippopotamus . . . Oh, excuse me, Miss . . ." Elaborately they passed by laughing, pushing one another into the bushes that bordered the sidewalk, turning and grinning widely at Bo.

She grinned back automatically, exhibiting her good nature like a white flag of peace, and Weezie by her side turned red. She stopped cold—Bo had to stop with her—and stared a moment. The two boys galloped ahead. Suddenly Weezie started off after them, yelling, ''YOU CREEPS, YOU FREAKS, YOU PINHEADS . . .'' and in her fury started to throw her books at them one by one . . . social studies . . . arithmetic . . . general science. ''FAT PEOPLE HAVE FEELINGS, TOO!'' General science hit one in the back of the leg. ''GOOD!'' Weezie yelled. ''IT SERVES YOU RIGHT!''

Bo, panting heavily, caught up with her. ''Stop it! Cut it out! It's all right!''

''No, it's not!'' Weezie turned on her. Her face was still red and now there were tears. ''How can you say that? It's not okay. It's awful. How come you don't know that?''

''Look, Louise, I appreciate it, but you don't have to fight my battles for me.''

''Yes I do. You never will.''

The expression on Weezie's face five years ago was essentially the same today. ''. . . And with Annette cheering him on it's disgusting. Every mean thing he says she giggles at. She doesn't know he calls her cone-chest behind her back. He's the one who started all those nasty nicknames.''

''Look,'' Bo said. ''If Marvin needs to do that to build himself up, it's just sad.''

''It's more than sad,'' Weezie protested. ''It's rotten.''

''You have to try to understand where people are coming from.''

''The trouble with you is you understand too much.''

''The trouble with you, Weeze, is you know the trouble with everything.'' It was as close to a criticism as Bo had ever come, and Weezie looked first surprised and then annoyed.

"Well, stop the world, and I'll get off." Bo said nothing. At Ash Street, Weezie started to turn off silently without looking back.

"Louise?" Bo called after her. She turned. "See you tomorrow?"

"Of course," Weezie shrugged, walking backward. Then she gestured with fake-tired dramatics: "Tomorrow and tomorrow and tomorrow . . ." They'd seen the movie of *Macbeth* together at the library in June, the night before Weezie went to camp. She sighed and gave Bo a half smile.

"Right." Bo grinned. Weezie turned and walked toward home. Bo felt oddly comfortable. They were solid, was the one thing she knew. A Jack Spratt combination of good and ill will. After all, what are friends for?

5

"**A**ssignment I: Describe Yourself, Outside and In—"

I ought to be able to toss that off before dinner, Bo thought, and opened her notebook. But it was harder than she thought.

I am fifteen and I am fat. How's that for a start, Ms. Albersham?

I am fifteen and I am slightly obese.

I am fifteen and I am pleasantly plump, twice. Marvin had said that to her in the seventh grade. "You're not fat, Butter—I mean, Barbara. You're pleasantly plump. Twice." She'd never figured out whether he was trying to be nice or rotten. She liked to give people the benefit of the doubt. She was beginning to resent Ms. Albersham, though. She hadn't signed up for creative writing to write about herself.

I am fifteen and I am gross.

"That's not so," she said out loud. "If it was so then certain people would not have behaved so decently to me."

Her stomach growled. A smell of garlic floated upstairs. Pasta, probably. Good. Bo banged the book shut and went to the top of the stairs. "Ma," she called down, "when is supper?" After a moment her little sister Reenie's voice came up. "She says ten minutes."

Bo sighed, went back to her room, and flopped down on her bed. What could you get done in ten minutes, after all? Anyway, she was tired of fighting it. She lay back, closed her eyes, and switched on her mental video. They were still there, the two of them, safely in the fourth row, reading through the script, Howard wearing that incredible, affable, lovable look.

• • •

"Ooooh, rough!" she read from the script and mimed her cheek against his.

"You're supposed to rub your cheek against mine. It says right there."

"Well, I will. This is just a run-through, I thought," she said, trying not to look embarrassed.

"There something wrong with my cheek?" he said innocently.

"Of course not."

"Then let's do it right." She did so. His cheek wasn't rough.

"You know, you're the one who's the sport," she said when they finished. She was afraid he might just walk away.

"How so?" he wondered.

Doing this with me, dummy. "Getting up on stage with a freshman," was what she said out loud. Not just a freshman, a fat freshman. "Playing straight man."

"Oh, that," he said. She noted that his eyes were very blue. "Well, it's kind of a tradition in the frosh show. Didn't Tippy explain?"

"Explain what?" Tradition to have a fatty make a fool

of herself? All fatties know it's tradition. It's required in fact. For life.

"In the freshman, excuse me, freshperson show," Howard continued, "they always have one upperclassman stick his head in somewhere. Like Alfred Hitchcock showing up in his own movies, you know? Only here it's somebody that the kids all know." He added modestly, "Maybe from sports or something."

. . . Or basketball or track or debate club or German club or council or science honors—how do I know so much about him?

"And they stick him in one of the comedy sketches—maybe a chorus line or something. Just stick him onstage here and there until it's sort of a running joke. Every time he's there and he's recognized the audience yells and screams."

"You mean," she said, beaming with her best nature, "you're going to upstage me?"

"Do you mind?" he asked with a straight face.

"Don't you? I mean the whole business."

He thought a minute, considering it. "If I said no, I'd be a rotten sport." He must have seen her face cloud because he added quickly, "But I'm glad I didn't. It's fun and I wouldn't have met you." A golden grin, platonic of course, but setting a glow in her. "And, anyway, it's nice to be the guy they pick. Almost an honor. A weird honor, but nice."

Was he going to leave? She had to make the conversation last. She said quickly, "You like honors?"

"Sure. I collect them."

I know.

"Not for myself, mind you." He smiled, kidding himself. "My mother keeps them stacked up on the mantel. My Howard's seventh grade bowling trophy. Howie's Mr. Congeniality certificate. She had it framed but never hung it up.

It's just sort of propped up there. Those are more or less recent, see. But she's got everything—my second grade perfect attendance medal—up there, and some stuff from camp way back when.''

''On the mantel?''

''Well, yeah. She likes to keep things out so she can find them. Why does she need to find my honors? Beats me.''

''Don't you mind?''

''What's to mind?''

''I don't know. I got a medal once for a composition I wrote and my mother made such a big deal of it, it started to bother me. . . . Do you have brothers or sisters?''

''Uh-uh. You?''

''Sister.''

''Older? Younger?''

''Smaller,'' Bo said. ''Little kid.'' She indicated her sister's height with her hand. ''Very cute.''

He raised an eyebrow, seeming to understand everything she meant without her saying half of it.

''SHAVING COMMERCIAL ONSTAGE,'' Tippy called.

''That's us.'' He smiled. Bo began to breathe perceptibly hard. ''Don't be scared,'' he said. ''We'll knock 'em out.'' He squeezed her hand. More than the warmth on her cheek, which after all was called for by the script.

Even now, months later, she was still aware of the place.

''Buttterrrr,'' Reenie was yelling. ''Come and get it!'' She meant dinner. Bo got up and headed downstairs. Dinner was about the only thing, of the things she wanted, that she was likely to get.

In the kitchen a smell of oil and garlic and tomatoes wrapped around her. Please let there be meatballs. She hated the vegetarian money-saving kind.

"Where's Daddy?" she said, peeking into the sauce pot. There were, thankfully, meatballs.

"Late," her mother said, averting her face as she dumped the contents of the pasta pot into the sink. Steam rose.

"He's always late," Reenie said. Bo looked at her mother's face, which was a careful blank.

"Don't exaggerate, creampuff," Bo said. "You tend to exaggerate." Bo tended to protect her mother.

"What's exaggerate?"

"Hand me the olive oil, will you please?" Her mother was running cold water over the pasta. The oil was on the counter very close to Reenie, who was now standing on one foot and looking out the window. Bo crossed the kitchen and brought the bottle back.

"What's exaggerate?" Reenie asked again.

"You know, don't you?" Bo said, handing her mother the oil.

"If I knew, why would I ask?" Reenie said in a sing-song chant she liked to use.

To keep the conversation centered on you, small one, Bo thought uncharitably and was immediately ashamed.

"Exaggerate means to make things too big," she said. "Overtell. Overkill, as it were." Her mother applied a spoonful of oil to the pasta and smiled slightly. "Come here." Bo beckoned to her sister. Reenie moved to her and Bo tucked the shirt all the way around the tiny waist of her sister's jeans.

"Maybe I want it out," Reenie said.

"Do you? I can put it out. Just be consistent, whichever."

"*I* can pull my own shirt out."

"So go ahead."

"I want it in."

"Fine." Bo gave her a mock spank on the bottom. "So," Bo said, "are you going to tell us all about it?"

"About what?"

"About school. How was it?"

"I don't know."

"She goes to kindergarten for the first time and she doesn't know?"

"It's the same as nursery school, just about, except they have more blocks." Bo and her mother exchanged a delighted look.

"What about *you*, love?" her mother asked Bo quickly. She was very careful about equal time. "How was *your* day? As I remember, nothing much happens the first day." Bo had often noted that Ruthanne Barrett had a habit of answering some of her own questions. "How's your schedule?"

"Passable," Bo said.

"Is your teacher awful?" Reenie asked. "Mine has this real curly red hair."

"Teachers. I've got more than one."

"So do I. I have two. One's more important, though."

"Reenie, your sister was telling us."

"She was?"

"Go on, please," her mother said to Bo as she ladled sauce onto three plates. "We can sit down now. Your father said he didn't know how late . . . oh, would you rather have your salad first? I could do that."

"*I* could do that, Ma, but I won't. I'll eat what you guys are eating. I've been smelling it for an hour."

"Oh, honey." Her mother looked stricken. "I didn't mean to make it harder."

"It's okay. I'm not trying right now."

"Nobody said you should."

Nobody ever did. The little innuendos: *"Salad first?"* Three slices of bread set out for four people. *"Oh, did you want butter, Butter . . . ?"*

"I don't think now's a good time," Ruthanne said,

giving her a supportive smile. "Too much stress. I mean with school starting again."

"Is there cheese?" Bo asked. Reenie passed her the green-foil cylinder. "We should get the real stuff sometime, like they have at Weezie's. They've got this little grater they pass all around . . ."

"With real Parmesan in it, no doubt"—her mother's voice thinned out slightly—"at nine dollars a pound, I'll bet."

"You've got sauce on your chin, Bobo. And up here." Reenie pointed to just below her nose. Bo applied her tongue to her upper lip and her napkin to her chin.

"How's that? And why aren't you eating, kiddo?"

Reenie took a spoonful and put it down. "It's hot."

"Blow on it."

"When will they give us work to do?" Reenie asked suddenly.

"Huh?" said Bo.

"In school. Homework."

"Oh, not this year I wouldn't think, ducky," her mother said. Bo saw the love all over her face, like tomato sauce. "Not in kindergarten."

"Right. This year you're supposed to learn to relate," Bo said, reaching for the bread.

"What's that?"

"What's which?"

"Relate."

Bo thought a moment. "It's sort of the same as exaggerate, but it has to do with people." Her mother looked up, startled.

"Barbara, don't confuse your little sister," she said.

Bo shrugged and lathered margarine on her bread. A small silence ensued into which her mother's ever-boundless enthusiasm leapt. "So, *tellll*," she said breathily.

"Me?" Bo said.

"You of *course*. How do your classes shape up? You probably can't tell yet. Is there anybody wonderful?" Ruthanne also had a way of saying wonderful with a suggestive little hum on the n: wonnnderful? In this instance she clearly meant, are there any cute boys? Her mother, poor soul, never gave up the notion that a fat girl might be perfectly attractive to cute boys. Bo sighed inside and chose to misread her.

"One good teacher," she said. "She's new. For creative writing."

"*Writing!* I'd forgotten you were doing that. Is that in place of English?—Reenie, don't do that." Reenie was burrowing under the mound of pasta with her fork and extracting spirals without sauce. "The nutrition's mostly in the sauce." Reenie made a face. "Is it?" Ruthanne directed to Bo.

"In the sauce?" Bo said.

"In place of English."

"No, I'm taking both," Bo said between bites.

"Well, that makes sense. You're so good at those things."

"Mommy, can I be excused?"

"What about your salad, Irene?"

"I don't want any."

"Take a vitamin, then. Dessert? It's your favorite."

"I'll wait for Daddy." Her mother sighed and nodded. Reenie slid off her chair and out of the kitchen.

"Annnyway . . ." Ruthanne addressed her older daughter again, with the expectant little hum on the n. "Where were you? Writing. What's she like, the new teacher?"

"Young. Well, youngish."

"Pretty?"

"I don't know. I guess she's attractive. It doesn't seem to matter."

"Of course not. But she's nice?"

"She's . . . different. Laid-back, sort of."

"Bo, honey, I really hate that expression. It sounds so . . ."

"Dirty or something?" Her mother colored slightly. "It just means *relaxed*."

"So say relaxed. Good writers don't use slang." Ruthanne beamed.

"Well, she's relaxed then. No, that's not quite it. Never mind. She's sort of . . . comfortable? At least she acts that way. She is pretty, actually, and very into the idea of writing, and she says really neat things about it. Her name is Ms. Albersham but she lets us call her Ms. A."

"Ms. . . . of course." Her mother's voice had thinned out again, but she held on to the same clear smile. "Does she have credentials?"

"I don't know. I suppose so."

"Well, I hope they hired someone with credentials."

There was a curious little silence for a moment.

"This sauce is fantastic, by the way," Bo said.

"Oh, really? It's just the usual."

Bo smiled and ate a little faster. There was another little silence.

"What will you write?" her mother asked, to fill it.

"I don't know yet," Bo answered, feeling tired. "She wants us to keep a journal and she gives these strange exercises."

"Oh? What are *they*?" Ruthanne was riveted again.

"I've only done one. They're . . ." Bo was cut off by her mother's look of satisfaction as she heard a car door slam.

"Well, it's about *time*." Ruthanne flashed Bo a you-know-him smile and got up. "At least I won't have to Seal-A-Meal his dinner again. I hate to waste those bags. I'll just put a flame under this. Will you have some more with your father?"

"Sure. Maybe I'll go call Weeze while you're doing that. I'll make it short."

"Whatever," her mother said, smiling and spooning sauce.

As Bo closed the kitchen door behind her, she heard the muffled sound of her father's voice. Her mother's voice sailed over it. "No! Tell!"

Howard Nevelson struggled for breath and woke up. Gibson, all fifteen pounds of him, was sitting on his chest. He shifted his body slightly to the left. The cat gave him a dirty look and rolled off, flicking his tail across Howard's face in the process. There was a note on the pillow fixed to the edge with an office clamp: "Grad seminar; home 9:00 or so." Howard removed the note, tucked the pillow under his head, and closed his eyes again. He had the sense of having dreamed but had no memory, just the physical sensation of having been elsewhere, less encumbered. He strained for it and crossed back over into sleep, but the place was darker than he expected.

The feeling under his feet was familiar, gym floor, and the breathing and clattering meant there were other players. He heard a *whish* and instinctively caught the ball, bounced it, and tossed it where the basket would be, though he was only guessing in the dark. He was dancing and sweating and, apparently from the noise, scoring occasionally. *Thud . . . thump . . . whish* . . . roar . . . *thud . . . thump* . . . time-out. His mouth was dry. He moved blindly to the sidelines. Someone gave him a cut orange to suck. *Thud . . . thump* . . . he moved back toward the sound. *Whish* . . . he felt the ball move past him again, had the sense it ricocheted, came back in his direction, passed him by. He tried to go where he thought it was, but his legs were stopped, fixed in place. He woke up again to find Gibson sitting on his feet.

"Could I have the light on tonight?" Reenie sat on the edge of the bed in summer pajamas.

"I guess so. How come?" Bo asked.

"I'm afraid."

"What of?"

"I don't know."

I know the feeling. "There's nothing to be afraid of, pumpkin."

"Would you sing?"

"One song. Which one?"

" 'Saturday Morning.' "

Bo sang:

"Come Saturday morning
I'm going away with my friend.
We'll Saturday spend till the end
of the day."

Reenie closed her eyes and listened. Bo thought she was asleep, and when she'd finished singing snapped out the light.

"No . . . please . . ."

"Okay." Bo snapped it on again. " 'Night, Reen."

"Bo?" she whispered. "Who's your friend?"

"You are, cooky."

It was the right answer.

6

*B*y the end of the first week of school, Bo was going crazy. Howard still hadn't turned up. Furthermore, something miraculous had happened. She'd found out he was going to be in her typing class.

"I almost died on the spot," Bo said to Weezie over the phone. "I mean, there Miss Costello was reading the computer sheet and once she'd called my name I sort of checked out, so to speak, so all of a sudden there's this silence, and then she says real loud, as though she's saying it again, 'Nevelson? Howard?' My stomach turned over. I mean, I was even thinking about him at the time."

"How unusual," Weezie said dryly. "So why do you think he's taking typing? Quick credit? Seniors do that sometimes."

"Howard wouldn't."

"Holy Howard? Heavens, no!"

"Please don't do that to me, Louise," Bo begged. "I'm in a weakened condition."

"God knows," Weezie said. "Weak in the head."

"Look," Bo said, "do you realize how wonderful this is? I mean, Howard Nevelson, two times a week, in my own class."

"Yeah, I suppose." Weezie softened a little. "But you really ought to opt for reality now and then, you know? I mean, I worry about you."

Bo got as lofty as she could, over the phone. "If you think," she said, "that I harbor any delusions about a future for Howard Nevelson and me as anything but nodding acquaintances . . ."

"I'd like it better if you did," Weezie said.

"Don't be stupid. Sometimes I just don't get you."

Weezie sighed loudly in Bo's ear. "All I'm saying, dear, is nobody is as wonderful as you think he is."

"Well, he's wonderful enough!" Bo practically yelled into the phone. Weezie sighed again. "Anyway," Bo said, "have you heard anything? I mean about where he is?"

"No mention whatsoever," Weezie said. "His absence doesn't seem to be obsessing anybody but you."

"It just feels so weird," Bo groaned, "not seeing him." She heard another sigh. "Look," she said as nicely as she could, "do me a favor, would you?"

"Such as?" Weezie asked.

"Take a walk with me. Now."

"You mean . . . you've got to be kidding. Give me a break, will you?"

"Weeze . . ." Bo implored. "Please?"

"I must be out of my gourd," Weezie said. "Ten minutes?"

"Bless you," Bo said, and hung up.

By the time they were approaching Butler Street Bo had their story all figured out. "Just in case we . . . just in case we run into someone we know, we're visiting Michelle Landaker. She lives down at the end of the street."

32

"Who is Michelle Landaker?" Weezie asked.

"I made her up," Bo replied. "She goes to Catholic school."

"Won't whoever we run into know she doesn't live here?"

"She just moved in."

"What does her father do?" Weezie asked, as if she really wanted to know.

"Please be quiet," Bo said, her voice becoming reverent. "That's his house." She nodded toward number 23. "Isn't it nice?"

"Looks like a house to me," Weezie said.

Bo kept to the right and kept her eyes straight ahead as they passed at a moderate speed. "Okay, what do you see? Just look as if you're not looking."

"I see . . . a bookcase and a lamp and a . . . picture of some sort . . ."

"It's a mirror," Bo corrected her.

"Incredible," Weezie said, straight-faced. "And all made of solid gold."

"Oh, shut up."

Louise looked at her friend, saw real pain, and stopped teasing. "Sorry. So did you figure anything out?"

"Yes," said Bo. "They're home."

"How do you know?"

"There's a light in the kitchen. And there's trash in the cans. I saw it out of the corner of my eye."

"You're amazing," Weezie said. "Now what?"

"We walk down to Michelle's house and when we see she isn't home, we proceed down the block out the other end and go home."

"Do not pass Go, do not collect two hundred dollars," Weezie said solemnly. "Which one is Michelle's house?" Bo picked out a darkened house toward the end of the block and they moved in its direction.

7

The following Wednesday, before the bell, Bo made her usual pilgrimage to 2N. She'd stopped trying not to. The hallway was crowded, but she would have picked out Howard instantly. She would have sensed his presence before she even saw him, wouldn't she? He wasn't there. Was it really going to be another whole week?

Her bladder blazing, she ducked into the girls' room and made for a stall. A few minutes later she heard two voices. The first, high-pitched and shaky, she couldn't identify.

"So he's back. I can't believe it. Really."

The second, throaty and gorgeous, unmistakably belonged to Cyndy Randall. "Now you know." The low voice was shaky, too.

"Why didn't you ever say?" the unknown voice asked.

"How could I?" Cyndy said.

"I thought . . . you know what I thought? I thought, she isn't talking because breaking up was so traumatic. I won't ask. You notice I didn't ask."

"It was traumatic. Don't you think it was? Under the circumstances? I mean, it would have been, anyway, but . . ." Bo strained to hear, holding her whole body rigid. Would they notice a door closed a long time? Stay quiet. What circumstances?

"Look," the high voice said. "Nobody is going to blame you. I'd've done the same thing. Anybody would. I mean, really . . ."

"Let's get one thing straight, Allison." Cyndy's voice became stronger. "*I* did not break it off. He came back at the end of August. He'd stopped writing, but I hadn't. I was the one who called. He'd never talk. I would have been humiliated, but I thought it was still all about his mother. Okay, I thought. It takes time. Be patient, Cynthia. Two years of a relationship don't just blow away because one person has a tragedy. One person needs the other even if he won't say so. Right? A whole relationship can't just vanish."

"You wouldn't think so," the voice identified as Allison offered. "You wouldn't think—"

"He wouldn't talk," Cyndy went on. "He wouldn't return my calls. So I went over there. He answered the door."

"Oh, wow," Allison started, "you—"

Cyndy cut her off. "*Not me,* got it?" Her words became distorted briefly, to Bo's anxious annoyance She must be putting on lipstick. "'Afther the ock or off, I though, is osn't aff oo he the end . . . I thought, okay, Cynthia, so what? We can fix it. I'll help. But he wasn't having any."

"Look," Allison said after a moment. "This is going to sound awful, Cyn, but maybe . . . maybe it's just as well?" In the stall, Bo held her breath.

"I suppose it is," Cyndy allowed. "I probably couldn't have done it. I'm no saint. He knows that. I mean, he knows *me*. I thought I knew him. Now I don't know . . ."

"So he set you free. It's kind of beautiful in a way."

There was a small silence. Cyndy must have glared at Allison, who said, "I just mean, oh, I don't know . . . I'm glad you've got Larry."

"Larry's been sweet," Cyndy said. Bo felt a stab of confused fury. "But we're keeping it light. We have to. One more year and I'm heading for Northampton, Mass. Smith."

"You're doing early decision?"

"Well, Howard wanted Amherst and so I got all gung ho about Smith. If they take me, of course."

"Don't be silly. They'll take you."

"We'll see. Anyway, I'm not going to change my plans just because of Howie. But I am not, repeat, not, getting that tied up with anybody again. Larry's nice to go with but that kind of pain again, no thank you. No serious relationship. Not for years."

"Look," Allison said slowly. Bo heard their footsteps on the tile floor. "The odds against something like this happening again . . ." The door closed off her voice.

Bo sat very still a moment, trying to sort it out, then left the stall and went to wash her hands. What it all meant she couldn't fathom, but she did know one thing: Howard Nevelson was free. Unless there was somebody new. But if that had happened, wouldn't they have said so? If Howard had left Cyndy for another girl his nature would be to tell her so, simply and directly. No. If he broke off with Cyndy he had a reason, and Bo wasn't going to judge anything from hearing only one side and only half of that. But Howard was free. She looked in the mirror. Howard was free and so what? The warning bell rang and she made a dash for homeroom.

She slipped into homeroom as the final bell rang. Palmer, staring out the window, didn't notice, of course. *Dong*. Dr. Jackson's voice came over the P.A. System. *"Please rise. 'I pledge allegiance . . .'"* If he's back . . . if he's really back, it could be . . . *"'One nation . . .'"* Prickles on her neck . . .

36

" '*Under . . .*' " Please. " '*God . . .*' " Stomach tightens . . . bladder objects . . . " '*Liberty and justice for all.*' " Justice demands it has to be . . .

"*Good morning. This is Howard Nevelson with your morning announcements.*" There was a mild ripple over homeroom. Bo saw stars.

She made a cradle with her arms and lay her head down in it, endeavoring to look bored and sleepy, but basking in the sound of him:

Photography club meets tonight in room two thirty-seven at seven P.M.
Girls who are interested in signing up for archery should be at the gym no later than three-fifteen today . . .

Things seemed so absolutely right. Up front Palmer curled the straggly hair around her finger and stared. In the first row Annette Morisi, her compact propped up on her notebook, put on lipstick and blotted, put on some more and blotted it again. Across the hall in the other sophomore homeroom Weezie was probably scowling at Marvin Newton. Back further in the room Sanford Yellen watched Mary Katherine longingly and Darlene counted the words in her English composition.

Somewhere in a kindergarten room Irene Samantha was learning to share. At home her mother was probably filling Seal-A-Meal bags. At work her father was telling his secretary what to do. The world spun on, doing beautifully. Howard Nevelson was back in school.

The only problem was living through the day until typing class. The bell released her into the hall. Weezie came up behind her. "What's wrong with you, as if I didn't know."

"Nothing's wrong. Everything's right."

"Superhero's back. And there she goes, space fans, up, up, and over the boundaries of reality . . ."

37

Bo just smiled. "Who is to say what reality is, much less where its boundaries are."

"You," Weezie said, "are not making any sense."

"Oh, I don't know, Weeze. Maybe not. All I know is I'm happy. Don't knock it."

"For as long as it lasts," Weezie said sourly.

"Why shouldn't it last? Fantasies last as long as you let them."

"You are positively poetic today, aren't you?"

"I'm inspired," Bo said.

Weezie groaned. "See you later."

The day ticked along, refusing to be rushed. Biology. She mangled a surprise quiz. Geometry. It all seemed senseless. She couldn't see the constructions on the board, but kept focusing on odd little details: the crepe soles of Darlene's shoes; the back of Weezie's hair, straight under the inflicted curl; Palmer's hands, still shaking. Even English, where she usually shone, failed to hold her. Finally the bell rang for lunch.

Bo hurried. If things went well and nothing got in her way, she could pass him at his locker.

It wasn't to be. As she passed by Ms. Albersham's room, the familiar voice rang out, "Barbara? Oh, good." Bo stopped. Ms. Albersham was smiling. "I was hoping I might see you before our next class."

"That's tomorrow," Bo said, trying hard to focus. She glanced down toward the end of the hall. The passing students were thinning out. Howard wasn't at his locker. A fat boy was bending over the drinking fountain.

Ms. Albersham was still smiling at her in an unthreatening way. "If it's about assignment three," Bo began, "I'll have it in tomorrow."

"Assignment—oh, no. I said I want all of you to work at your own pace, didn't I?"

"My pace is awfully slow, I know," Bo said.

"There was Mozart, and there was Brahms," Ms. Albersham said. Bo wondered vaguely what they had to do with it. Ms. Albersham didn't explain. Instead she said, "Could you come by after your last class today? If not, we could meet another time."

"I . . . yes, sure," Bo said. "If there's a problem."

"No, no problem. Did I say there was a problem? I'd just like to discuss something." Bo was baffled, but she agreed and hurried off. Hardly anyone was left in the hall. Thank God it was lunchtime.

When she got to the cafeteria she ordered and ate the balanced lunch, as well as the one her mother had packed for her.

She limped through fifth and sixth period. Sixth was the worst. Study hall. Study what? For months she'd been waiting for Howard and Howard was at hand, next class. She sighed, pulled out her biology assignment, and attempted to draw the required diagram of a paramecium making itself into two. But her pencil had a life of its own and when she looked down she was startled to see not a paramecium but a pair of wide shoulders which she recognized, even though she didn't draw well, as belonging to Howard's torso, the way it had looked that night on stage.

For the show itself he'd pared down to a T-shirt and jeans. She'd seen that much of him before—more in fact, on the basketball court—but never so close. His body was wonderful-looking. The warm feeling she sometimes had when she thought about him was starting. She clenched her knees against it. It was going to be hard enough, a half-hour from now, just to say hello. She'd wanted to put her hands all over him but the script only called for their linking elbows. Then the best part, she was to rub her cheek elaborately across his, grimace, and squeal, "Ooooh, rough!" and later, after she'd daubed his face with Cool Whip and he'd gone offstage briefly, supposedly to shave with "Saylor's Super Shave Cream" (the chemistry teacher's name was Saylor), she got to rub his cheek again and proclaim "Mmmm-smooth." Whereupon the assembled student body, parents, relatives, and teachers broke up.

Why was it funny? Because of who they were and what she looked like. Because everybody was primed to laugh. And because there was something shiny and wonderful and good-natured about Howard Nevelson, and when she was next to him, about her, too. How could she convey to anyone (and did she want to?) that he had conferred on her acceptability. Not just by her classmates, but by herself.

Bo erased the shoulders and tried to make Howard into an acceptable example of parthenogenesis. About eighteen hours later the bell rang. Her stomach jumped. Seventh period. Typing. Him.

She stayed back a minute, letting everybody go ahead out the door, then made for the girls' bathroom. She didn't look in the mirror, but laid her stack of books on one side of a sink, and straightened them carefully. Two pages were falling out of her ring binder, looking sloppy. She opened it and tucked them back. She arranged the books smallest to largest and put her pencil case on top. Then she looked in the mirror. "Nitwit," she addressed herself. "What are you trying to do?" She turned sideways and took the clips out of her hair and tipped her head back. Her mother always said her hair was her best feature. Bo wished, though, that she didn't sound so wistful when she said it. She looked sideways at herself again. Her hair reached down her back. She took out her hairbrush and applied it, but the hair rose in staticky drifts. "Nitwit," she said again. Her bladder protested but she knew it was a fraud. She let the hair lower itself and picked strays off her collar, then put the clips back. She pulled at a paper towel, swore when it stuck, pressed the lever to allow another six inches out, pulled it off, ran it under cold water and over her face. Droplets lodged on her upper lip. She ran a hand under the back of her hair, picked up her books, and pushed the door open with them.

The hall was nearly empty. A couple stood outside a classroom gazing at each other in a way that made Bo look down in embarrassment. It was curiously quiet as she moved quickly toward typing class. She could feel the droplets of water drying on her face, but a cold sweat was on her neck and inside her elbows.

Up ahead the fat boy she'd seen earlier was moving slowly, looking at room numbers. He must be new, she thought. Why did I spend so long in the bathroom. Now I've got to make an entrance. Howie right there in the front desk. Do I nod? Do I say "Hi"? Do I say "I'm glad you're back"? No, not there in front of everybody. Just hi, but convey with a look that I'm glad he's back? A platonic look, of course. She was moving fast but trying to keep from perspiring any more. Miss Costello's room was at the end of the hall. The fat boy was now a few lockers ahead of her. A transfer, he must be. Welcome, fellow fatty. There are at least half a dozen of us now. Maybe we can have a club. *"Fatties' club meets on Tuesday at three-fifteen for election of officers . . ."* She could hear Howard's voice matter-of-factly making the announcement.

She was nearly up to the new boy now. There was something familiar about the back of his neck. He stopped abruptly, and she nearly barreled into him as he turned into Miss Costello's typing class.

The fat boy was Howard Nevelson.

8

*B*o stumbled into Miss Costello's room in shock, afraid for a moment she hadn't said hello, just stared. "Bo. Hi," the fat boy said in Howard's voice. But she must have performed all right. Performing was one thing she was used to. It came with the body. There was time for no more than, "Hi, Howard . . . I'm glad you're back," and the friendliest of smiles before the bell rang. Had she managed? How had she looked? Who was this Howard and where was the one she knew?

Miss Costello had set up the record player and had them typing to music while she spent time trying to bring Howard up to date. "You've missed the fundamentals," Bo heard her say crossly, as "The Japanese Sandman" played, marked rhythmically by the sound of nineteen typewriters and the whole class chanting a-s-d-f-shift, a-s-d-f-shift.

"Somebody isn't keeping time," Miss Costello raised her voice over them. It was Bo, who kept hitting between the keys as she tried not to look at Howard's back, his shirt straining over it.

The worst of it was following him out of class and down the hall, watching people react. Some who had seen him earlier said loud good-natured hi's while nudging whoever they were walking with. Faces wore hidden shock, open shock, careful control, unsuccessful control. And some of them passed him right by because they didn't recognize him at all. And if he said hi, which he was doing as if things were normal, some would turn suddenly and look back and give one of those oh-my-God-is-that-really-you-Howie looks that were the worst of all. No, worse even was an occasional betrayal of malice, a mean little gleam of "and you always thought you were hot stuff, Nevelson."

Bo had absorbed all of this, walking behind him. There was a point where she could have turned, should have, and gone up the stairway and to her locker, thrown in her books, found Weezie, and limped home. But somehow she felt obliged to stay behind him, receiving it all, as if she could attract some of his pain and let him suffer the less. She knew then that she would have to keep doing that if she could. If it happened that he would let her.

She was taking the longest drink of water she could manage at the fountain on 2N when she remembered she was supposed to be somewhere else. She arrived pink-faced and breathless and started to say, "I'm sorry . . ." when Ms. Albersham stopped her.

"Whoa, Barbara, wait a minute. May I make a suggestion? It's a poor policy in life to begin every encounter with an apology," she said.

"Oh . . . I'm . . ." Bo began and stopped, not knowing what to say if she couldn't say "I'm sorry."

"You're not late, you know. I said after class, no particular time. But even if you were, it wouldn't be worth the look of total tragedy you're wearing." Ms. Albersham smiled warmly. Bo smiled back automatically, without feel-

43

ing it. Ms. Albersham must have guessed, because she looked at her more closely. "Now *I'm* sorry. Sometimes I leap to conclusions. Are you okay, hon?"

"I'm fine," Bo said. "I just got some bad news about a friend."

"That's too bad," Ms. Albersham said. "Would it help to talk about it?"

"No," Bo said quickly. "I mean, thanks, but no." Talking about it would make it real, she felt. Maybe she'd been hallucinating. Maybe if she didn't mention it Howard would be his old self tomorrow.

"Okay." Ms. Albersham didn't seem offended. "I guess you want to know why I wanted to talk to you." Bo squinted. She'd already forgotten she'd been asked to come. "The Japanese Sandman" was playing loudly in her head . . . a-s-d-f-shift.

"Two things, actually," Ms. Albersham went on. "In the first place, I want to say that I've been enjoying your work. Just from these first assignments it's clear you have talent." She paused.

Bo had heard what she said, but there seemed to be a time lapse, as if the words had traveled a long way to reach her. Finally she managed, "Thank you."

"What you've turned in so far," the teacher continued, "has been sweet-tempered but insightful. There's imagination and, more important, honesty, there. Yes . . . it's good. You could be good." Light rays were coming at a slant through the window, dust dancing in them. It reminded Bo of the lights on the stage that night, bright rays full of dust, blinding them to the audience. The light hit Howie's white T-shirt, stretched over his muscles. He'd looked like something in an art book. "You could be good, of course," Ms. Albersham was saying, "if you're willing to work. It's always a risk, telling people they have talent. Sometimes they think that's enough. Especially young people. But I want you

44

to know what I think, because I'm going to be tough on you.'' She smiled. Bo looked blank.

"Also," Ms. Albersham went on, "I suspect you have some flair as a critic. Your remarks in class on what we've read have been astute, but tactful. Never mean. That's valuable. I'm always a little nervous when we put classwork up for discussion. Kids—I mean young people—can be pretty rotten in what they say. And that can be destructive."

"I know," Bo almost whispered. "It's awful." She was thinking of the faces that Howard had had to face, walking down that hall.

"Which brings me to my second point," Ms. Albersham said. "Just a notion, in its infancy. I've been thinking about our doing a little literary magazine out of the work from my classes and perhaps from individual submissions. I guess it's been a while since Parkview has had one. I was thinking of involving you, maybe even as editor." Bo looked at her oddly. She appeared to be at the end of a tunnel. There was light behind her.

Ms. Albersham smiled again. "Yes, you," she said, as if Bo had asked. "I don't believe in this hierarchy-of-classes business. Actually, as a sophomore you'd probably have more time. What do you think?"

Bo wondered. For some reason she had the feeling she might be very busy this year. Very tied up. "I don't know," she said.

"And the idea makes you nervous, doesn't it?" Ms. Albersham looked at her kindly. "Well, nothing's definite at this point. I'd just like you to think about it. Will you?"

"Uh-huh. Yes. Sure," Bo said. She was desperate to get home now. She had a lot else to think about. Bo managed another thank you and a weak smile and started out.

"Barbara?" She felt Ms. Albersham's gentle hand on her shoulder. She turned. "I want to say . . ." Ms. Albersham fumbled a bit, then took a breath and a risk, "I want to say that I didn't tell you all that because you're overweight and I thought you needed to hear it." Bo's eyes widened. "I told you because it's true."

There was that time lapse again before the words reached Bo. Somewhere they felt good. She set them aside and wondered what Howard needed to hear.

9

*T*he following Monday Bo walked ahead of Howard out of class, but stayed near enough to catch the reactions that were still happening, the fast face-adjustments that said, Yeah, that's Nevelson, didn't I tell you?

She got to the corner, still aware of him at her shoulder, desperately trying to think of something to say for openers, when she heard the voice of last spring. "Bo?" She turned.

"Oh, Howard," she said. "I didn't know that was you," and wondered at the automatic little lie. She took a nervous breath and said, "I've been meaning to say I'm glad you're back."

"You did," he said.

"Did what?"

"Say that."

"I did?"

"Wednesday. The first day I hit school." He grinned a little. The word *hit* was loaded. He was sharing something with her. She felt honored and confused.

47

"Well, I meant it. You . . ." She wanted to say look good, another ordinary lie she'd heard her mother use a thousand times it seemed, whenever they met a friend she hadn't seen in a while, even if the friend looked awful. But Bo knew better than anybody how that particular lie could hurt. ". . . You . . . missed over a week," she concluded lamely.

"Right," he said, as if it were obvious why. "I've been meaning to tell *you* . . ." (Me? she thought, astounded.) "I wanted to thank you for your note, last spring. I appreciated it. Really."

"Oh." Bo wondered what else to say. "You must've got a lot of notes." Dumbo. Bimbo. Nitwit. What will he think you meant by that?

"Actually I didn't," he said simply. "A few. Not a lot. From around here, anyway."

"I guess maybe people didn't know what to say," she said, aware of wanting to protect him again. "I know everybody was sorry. It must have been awful." He said nothing, looking at her in a way she couldn't read. She went on, wanting to fill the space. "I guess it still is. I mean . . ." she fumbled.

"It was rough," he acknowledged. "A shock, you know?" He waited as if expecting her to add something. She swallowed.

"I guess you still miss her a lot. I know I would if it happened to me." How was that? Too frank? Too stupid?

"Well, yeah, I guess," Howard said after a moment. "But you get used to things. You can get used to anything, right?" He gave her the sharing look again. She looked back at him, a large puffed-up version of her Howard, as though someone had applied a bicycle pump to him. *Right?* She wanted to say *no*, but she nodded.

Later that week, when Weezie was out sick, he'd caught up with Bo walking alone. "Hey. Are you hungry?"

"Of course." She smiled.

They took a table up front at Mitch's. "What'll you have?" Howard asked.

Bo studied the laminated menu a moment, then felt silly because everybody knew what was on it—pizza or calzone, sausage sandwiches or burgers, french fries or onion rings. She was confused because she didn't know who was paying.

"I'm paying," Howard said, making her jump. She objected mildly, not wanting to insult him but wanting him to know she didn't consider this a datelike situation.

"No, I invited you," he said, confusing her further. "Next time we'll go dutch." Next time? She ordered a cheeseburger.

"Side of coleslaw?"

"Might as well live it up," she said.

"Fries?"

"Rings," she said, then remembered that Cyndy liked them and changed it. "No, fries are fine."

"Sure?"

"Yeah."

She was frantic until the food came, wondering how to be. He didn't seem to notice. He talked easily and asked a lot of questions. She remembered this from last spring, that when Howard Nevelson asked you a question he listened intently to you, put in his own experience, and added it up to something mutual. She was dazzled once again by his manner of equality. "What do *you* think?" he'd say, as if it mattered.

He also hit the big issues head-on. "So," he said at one point, "Parkview still seems to be in shock over the new me." He munched his burger. "Why do you think that is?"

She wished she could say, in the manner of her friend Louise: because those creeps haven't got anything better to do; because they're cruel and mean and stupid . . . but her own better nature stopped her. She frowned at her french fries a moment, trying to work it out. "I think," she said finally, "it has to do with status."

"Ah-hah," he said, as if that were clever of her, and waited for more.

"—I mean," she went on tentatively, "a nonentity who suddenly gets fat isn't anything but a fat nonentity. But a biggie like you—that's a fat phenomenon. If you follow me. And pardon the alliteration." She wondered if she'd gone too far.

Apparently not, because he grinned. It was hardly a new idea, but he found her willingness to talk about it disarming and likable. He said so, more or less.

She shrugged. "Listen, I've been facing fat all my life." And wanted badly to add: but I don't want it for you. It hurts too much and you don't deserve it. Why did you do such a thing, Howard Nevelson? You're not a bimbo like me.

"Would you rather be thin?" he asked.

"Of course," Bo said quickly, then seemed to reconsider. "All else being equal. Wouldn't you?"

He thought about it. "I don't know," he said, catching a trickle of catsup from the rim of his burger with his tongue. "Maybe not. Not for now."

"How come?"

"Because I'd have to stop eating." He smiled and signaled for Mitch. "Two more," he said, not asking her, waving at their plates. He said it loudly, she noticed, steeling herself against the glances from adjoining tables. He'd meant them to notice. She knew about that somewhere. Howard was performing, the way she had been, for years.

Somewhere part of Bo had known for quite a while that being fat was a lot of who she was. She didn't like that about herself, but it seemed to be the best she could do for now. But Howard already had an identity. So why was he sitting there in front of her, shoveling food down as if his life

50

depended on it? A bell went off in her head and she heard his voice from last spring. "She keeps my honors up there on the mantel . . ." Bo shook her head. It was too confusing.

She wasn't at all sure how she happened to be sitting there at Mitch's with Howard Nevelson, but she was sure of one thing: the assembled populars, in- and out-misfits, and nonentities who were there all thought it was because she was fatter than he was—at least for the present—although he was gaining on her rapidly. She blinked against the pun and the truth of it.

"What's the matter?" Howard asked.

"Something in my eye," she lied quickly.

"Let me see." He reached forward, drew the skin under her eyebrow up, and peered at her. His eyes seemed smaller than she remembered, but were the same startling blue.

"Blink," he said. She did so, fiercely. Her eyes watered. "That get it?"

"Yeah, I think so." Why are such lies as automatic as breath, she wondered. Trace them back to the first pretense, so often an impulse not to hurt somebody's feelings. What's wrong with that? Nothing, she supposed. But it got so complicated so fast you couldn't keep track of it. Still, she could be halfway honest with him. She could say the word fat to his face and acknowledge that he was, that something had happened, and changed the way people acted toward him. Though every last one of them, with the exception, maybe, of the basketball coach, would probably deny it.

There were shock waves at home, too.

"I'm sorry," Bo said as she came in. "I don't know how it got so late." She was trying to sound offhand, but she couldn't keep the stack of books in her arms together. "I was at Mitch's." The books landed in a chair, every which way.

"I figured," her mother said. She was hemming a pair of slacks. "I wasn't worried. You know I always trust you,

51

love." Bo did and it depressed her. "How is Weezie? Is her hair starting to grow in?"

"I wasn't with Weeze. She's sick. I was with a friend from last year."

"Oh. From choir?"

"A boy, actually."

Her mother's eyebrows flickered. She stitched faster and let herself smile carefully. She glanced at the heap of books and back at Bo, who had half turned around. "I guess it's time," she said. "Oh, my. My baby, dating boys."

Bo was irked. In the first place, it was way past time, and in the second place . . . "It wasn't a date, Ma," she said out loud.

"I see." Ruthanne had hemmed all the way around one leg of the slacks but appeared to be starting the same one over. "But you went out," was all she said.

"If you call Mitch's out."

"I do. You went out with a boy." The needle moved nervously.

"A boy can also be a friend," Bo said. "Not as in boyfriend."

"You're right, of course," her mother said, so sincerely that Bo knew she meant the opposite. "Who was it?"

"Howie Nevelson."

"*Howie Nevelson!* The boy from the show?" Bo had forgotten she would know him from "Mmmm-smooth" days.

"Yeah, that's the one." She swore she could feel her mother's heart pumping. The whole room seemed to expand and contract.

"The one whose mother died."

"Killed. She was killed."

"Poor thing. How is he?"

"He's changed some," Bo said and sat down.

"Well, you're bound to. Such a terrible thing. I'm thrilled you're seeing him."

Bo leaned back and looked at the ceiling in exasperation. Her voice became a chant: "I'm not seeing him, Ma. We went to Mitch's."

"Dear heart, I'm simply saying that there is a time in life when it's pleasant to have male company occasionally instead of exclusively female. I'm pleased you have arrived at that time. It doesn't have to mean dating, in the old-fashioned sense."

"Well, it isn't," Bo said and got up. "We're going to the movies Saturday," she tossed over her shoulder.

Ruthanne glistened. "Saturday *night*!" Bo sighed inside. She knew that in her mother's mind anything done on a Saturday night that wasn't done with girlfriends equaled a date.

"Saturday night. So?"

"Well, I *mean* . . ." her mother started and shifted. "I'm just surprised a boy like that . . . is free on a Saturday night."

Bo shook her head hopelessly. What did her mother think, anyway—that a Prince Charming had finally recognized the totally seductive female that lived under her padding? Or that he was into the beauties of her mind? But all she said was, "Well, it's not a date."

Her mother looked thoughtful. "I wonder if you should have your hair trimmed a little. Victor could maybe fit you in on Thursday after school."

10

Something mean in Bo wanted not to warn her mother. Let her expect the gorgeous golden Howie of last spring. Have the new large version of him make an entrance. Bo'd watch her face, watch it say, "No wonder," and struggle not to have it show. But for Howard's sake, Ruthanne had to be prepared. Bo couldn't allow him to watch that, too. So that Saturday night after supper she said, "Listen, there's something you'd better know, Ma." Ruthanne raised her eyebrows and looked expectant. "Howard has gained a lot of weight."

"Oh?" Her mother's face said nothing, with care.

"I mean a lot. He's fat now."

"Howard is." It wasn't a question, just a restatement of what Bo had said. Ruthanne's face looked odd for a moment, then what settled on it was surprising but unmistakable: pain. For whom? Bo wondered. For her? For Howie? For the pair they would be and the sheer embarrassment? And whose embarrassment, theirs or hers?

"Yeah," Bo said. "Howard." All of a sudden she couldn't cover anymore. She started to cry and she couldn't stop. Ruthanne opened her arms to her daughter and Bo moved into them, trying not to knock her over. Her mother held her as well as she could and rubbed her back and said, "Oh, baby, oh, love . . ." Bo sobbed and gulped and sobbed again. The pair of them rocked together.

When the sobs died down to sniffles her mother held her away gently and pushed at the hair that had matted on Bo's cheek. "People are people, love," she whispered. "People are people, no matter what. I've been telling you that for years."

"Damn straight," Bo said, and went upstairs to get ready.

She was rummaging through the medicine cabinet when there was a knock on the bathroom door.

"Butter?" It was Reenie. "Can I come in?"

Bo sighed to herself. Was there no place or time on earth that she was entitled to privacy? But she said, "Sure, Cracker Jack." Reenie opened the bathroom door but remained at the threshold. "Don't you have to use the john?" Bo asked.

"Uh-uh."

"Then why?" She tried not to be annoyed.

"I just wondered what you were doing."

And assumed, of course, that I would be delighted to see you, Bo thought, but said, "Actually, I'm looking for the aspirin."

"You know the aspirin isn't in there. It's in the linen closet in the sick box."

Bo knew. She was picking up odd-shaped bottles with flowered labels. "This has got to be the only medicine cabinet in town with no medicine in it. Wouldn't you think, just once, Ma could say no to the Avon lady?"

"She can't," Reenie said. "She told me. The Avon lady has five kids and no husband. I mean she had one, but he went somewhere."

"And he didn't say where," Bo said.

"I guess not." Reenie shrugged.

Bo picked up a yellow tube and studied it casually. "Hmmm. Lemon mint facial mask. Should she or shouldn't she?" She struck a questioning pose.

"Who's she?"

"Me! . . . Why not?" Bo said into the mirror and opened the tube.

"What are you doing?" Reenie asked.

"Beats me," Bo said. "Putting yellow glop on my face."

"Why?"

"Why indeed. To improve it, I guess. Fat chance. Ha-ha. Get it? Fat chance?"

Reenie looked serious. "I like your face anyway."

"Kumquat, if I didn't have muck all over me, I'd kiss you."

"Mama says you're going out with a boy."

"That's true." That is true. Bo stared at herself a moment, the yellow substance hardening on her face.

"On a date?"

"No, not a date. Did Ma tell you it was?"

"No. I thought when you went out with a boy that meant a date."

How, Bo wondered, did the kid pick up these things? Osmosis? Or did it pass through the genes. "Small one, get this: I'm going out to the movies with a boy who is a friend. Not a boyfriend."

"What's the difference?"

"There's a difference." Unfortunately, Bo thought.

Reenie tried to figure this out and failed. "Then why can't I come downstairs and see him?"

"Who said you can't?"

"Mama."

"I don't . . ." Bo started. "What did she tell you?"

"She said you were going out with a boy and should have privacy."

Bo was irritated and at the same time grateful. Her mother just couldn't get it through her head. Still, she said, "Well, I guess Ma must have her reasons."

"If you don't care, why should she?" Reenie said, reasonably.

"Beats me." Bo shrugged.

"Then do I have to stay upstairs when he comes?"

Bo looked at her sister. What was it she wanted to see? It wasn't as if the child were malicious. But couldn't Bo take something for herself, just her, just this once? ". . . Well, I guess you'd better, Reen," she said. "Stay up here, I mean."

"How come?"

" 'Cause Ma said so, didn't she?"

Bo, who had surprised herself, looked in the mirror and raised her eyebrows. The yellow mask cracked on her forehead.

She would have been startled to learn that Howard, precisely at that moment, was staring in his own bathroom mirror, scraping the blond stubble off the small area of his chin where it tended to sprout, and watching the face of the stranger. Although he saw him every morning, he was not yet accustomed to the enlarged person who had arrived bit by bit over the past months and who had apparently decided to stay.

"Looks are a bonus, love, that's all." When was it, maybe six months ago? He had been standing like this, frowning at a zit, having forgotten to close the bathroom door, when his mother had come up behind him, the top of her hair just clearing his shoulder.

• • •

She flung an arm over his shoulder and moved around him, a questioning look on her face. "Looks are a bonus, you know?" she said and handed him a bottle of medicated lotion. He applied it to the spot on his nose. "Not that I'm not grateful to have a beautiful child, but I'd hate for him to get a swelled head." She winked and leaned back against the tile, watching him. "Who are you taking out? Or is it none of my business?" It wasn't, he figured, but he never knew how to say so.

"Cynthia."

"Aaaah." The knowing look that always bugged him. "La Randall. Again. Is that a steady thing?"

"Maybe." He did his fake gangster bit. "You wanna make somethin' out of it?"

"Why should I object? The girl's got everything, right? Looks, brains, money . . . She's probably even moderately hot stuff . . . Whoops, I misspoke myself, sorry. . . . Look, the two of you make a gorgeous pair. Just, it's early times for pairing."

"I'm not exactly buying her a ring."

"Glad to hear it." She pinched the back of his neck and left.

As much as such conversations had annoyed him, he felt the lack of them now. Occasionally he ran one through his head in a fantasy, just for the heck of it.

"Who's the lucky girl tonight, love?" Her head came around the shoulder of the stranger. She handed him his razor.

"Name's Barbara. Barbara Barrett."

"Do I know her?"

"Um, you might remember her. Remember the girl I did the act with in the freshman show? Not my freshman year, hers. The show last spring. Last spring before you took your goddamn car and slammed it into a goddam wall . . ."

His hand was shaking. She had vanished. He brought her back, insisting: *"Last spring, the shaving act, that girl . . ."*

"That girl?" Her face was amazed and smiling. *"The funny little fat one?"*

"Barbara Barrett. Butter Barrett. Bo."

"Well, aren't you something else!"

"Not something, Ma. Somebody." But she couldn't seem to notice, even in his fantasy, what he really looked like. She never had.

"That girl . . ."

"You wanna make somethin' out of it?"

• • •

Ruthanne's eyes betrayed nothing as she made her gushy kind of small talk. "I will never, if I live to be a thousand, forget the two of you in that show. Will you, Stan?"

Stan Barrett was tacking down a strip of raised flooring. Just the sort of thing your normal father does at eight-thirty on a Saturday night, Bo thought.

"What? Oh, excuse me," he said. "This thing's been driving Ruthanne crazy. Keeps catching her bedroom slipper in it. Swears she'll sue me." He hastily wiped off a palm and shook Howard's hand. "Sure, I remember that one. You were both terrific. Of course, I thought my little girl stole the show."

"Oh, Daddy," Bo said on cue.

"So did I," Howard contributed as her mother beamed and blinked.

Ruthanne walked down the steps of the front hall with them and closed the door behind them. When her husband appeared with his hammer and a handful of tacks, tears were streaming down her face. "What's the matter? You wanted her to go out with boys, right?"

"Of course. It's just . . . I just . . . They look so . . ." She stopped, then managed, "they look so . . . young and vulnerable and I don't know." Reenie, who had galloped downstairs, squeezed between the two of them and peered out the glass in the door.

"Boy, are they ever fat," she said.

11

Monday night after dinner, Bo told her mother she was going to the library and headed out the front door. Then she backtracked to the garage and hoped the sound of the door sliding up the track wouldn't be noticed. Well, she hadn't said specifically she was going to the local branch, had she? Why should she feel guilty if her mother jumped to conclusions? Because you meant her to, and you know it, creep, a voice in her head said. "Oh, shut up," she said back to her conscience. "This is important."

She made her way back to her bike in the dark, pulled the cobwebs off it, and tried the light. It glowed weakly. "Good enough," she muttered. She wasn't so eager to attract attention, which was why she only used the bike when she absolutely had to, why she was now dressed in a black long-sleeved jersey and black jeans, a black scarf tied around her hair, and why she'd waited till dusk to make the trip.

She wheeled the bike forward. It creaked horribly. She found a can of something she knew her father used to lubricate things he was working on and sprayed it here and there on the bike, wherever it seemed logical. Then she half-wheeled, half-carried it down the driveway and partly down the block, put her shoulder bag in one of the side baskets, and tried to mount. The bike tipped dangerously to the left. Her feet came off the pedals as she tried to correct it and something sharp dug into one of her ankles, hard. She tried a second time, and careening a bit, she wobbled off, aware of how weird she must look and of the hardness of the seat, much too small for her posterior. Well, Kenview was only five miles away. Five miles! Parkview, Fairview, Kenview, Overview . . . the county fathers had some imagination, she thought, especially given that none of the townships had views. But at least in Kenview the librarian wouldn't know her or her mother and couldn't blab. The trip was a necessity. Something had to be done about Howard.

What she couldn't get over, on the date that was not a date, was that the person who had sat next to her at the movies and across from her at Mitch's afterward was still Howard. Under the new padding, somewhere there had to be the same muscles he'd had last year in the show—*the same ones*.

Actually, a lot of him was the same. He was still funny and wonderful. Funnier, in fact. He made jokes about himself that made her laugh because he expected it but made her hurt all the more for him inside.

Obviously his brain hadn't been affected. He'd dissected the movie, which they'd both hated, brilliantly. She'd held her own in that conversation, too. The memory made her smile and pick up speed on the bike. And again, just like last spring, he'd dazzled her by the way he'd listened to what she had to say.

He'd mentioned that now he'd be helping to coach basketball instead of playing. She couldn't tell if he minded when he said it. Maybe, she hoped, it was a relief to tell people how to compete, instead of having to do it himself. It would have been for her. But she wasn't Howard. They were nothing alike. Nothing. He'd gotten fat by mistake or out of self-defense or by reason of temporary insanity. Third-degree fat, she thought to herself as she pedaled on toward Kenview. So clearly the sentence had to be shorter. She would see to that herself, somehow. The first thing that had to be done was research.

An hour later she arrived, huffing and puffing, on the steps of the new Kenview Branch of the Mannowac County Public Library. She nosed the bike into the rack and sat down for a minute at the top of the steps, checking her watch. Good. She had at least an hour before the library closed, so she could take a few minutes to catch her breath. Her jersey was sticking to her all over, and she could feel sweat trickling down the back of her thighs, but there wasn't much she could do about it.

Her ankle throbbed. She looked down at her feet and saw that a large red blotch was hardening on her sock. She smiled slightly, feeling a curious satisfaction. It was the first blood she'd shed on behalf of Howard Nevelson. It gave her an odd sort of courage. She got up, pushed through the revolving door, and walked straight to the desk. She blanched slightly to find a college-age boy behind it but said, anyway, as confidently as she could, "I need everything you have on grief and fat."

He didn't even look up but continued to sort papers. He mumbled, "Card catalog," and pointed an elbow toward it. Bo was annoyed and for a change let it show.

"Excuse me," she said fairly loudly, "I'm in a rush. Where would I find the books on grief and fat?"

He looked up at her, met her eyes, and gave a little smirk. "Under G," he said precisely. "And under F. Over there." And he pointed again to the area of the card catalog. "You could also try D for death or deceased or defunct or O for obesity or obscene . . .'' He looked mean and pleased with himself.

Bo held on tight, fixed Howard in her mind, and spoke slowly and deliberately. "Could you tell me, so that I can save some time, what areas of the shelves have those topics—so that I can just go and scan the titles?"

"I could," he said. "Sure I could. My mind is a veritable computer full of library trivia. But I'm told our sacred mission here is not to lead the unenlightened through the intricacies of the system, but to produce library users capable of independent research."

"In the time you took to say that you could have told me," Bo said.

"In the time we've been altercating you could have looked under G or F or O," he gave back. His eyes were beginning to look a little wild.

"Do you treat everybody this way or just a select few?" Bo asked.

"You got it," he said.

"I thought so. Do you have a supervisor?" she said loudly.

"Do we have a problem?" a voice said suddenly. As if Bo had rubbed a bottle or something, a very fat woman appeared. The boy said a dirty word under his breath, loud enough for Bo to hear but not the woman, who was apparently his boss. She wore a name tag that said, M. Mobley, Head Librarian.

"I'm looking for books on death and obesity," Bo said. "I don't mean dying from it," she corrected. "I mean grief, uh, bereavement, and stuff, you know?—and then books about fat. Other books."

"I understand," the woman said, and gave Bo a look of melting kindness, head to toe. "And I'm sorry. It's hard enough to be going through difficulties, isn't it?" She sighed ı sigh that seemed to include the whole world. "Try sections

64

six thirteen, six sixteen, one fifty-five, and one seventy, just over there." She pointed a fat arm gracefully. The flesh hung down in wobbles. "And if you can't find what you want, let me know." Her voice was musical, and rather soothing. As Bo turned away she heard her reprimanding the boy, "Peter, can't you see that child is in mourning?"

Bo searched the shelves, found what she wanted, and came back to the desk with an armful of books. The boy was gone, and the fat-lady supervisor sat behind the desk. She checked Bo's books out and gave her another awfully kind look. "I'm sorry for your pain, dear," she said, and reached up to pat Bo's hand. Her eyes were full of knowing, so Bo couldn't very well correct her. "And I want to apologize for Peter. He has problems of his own."

"Everybody does, I guess," Bo said.

"Too true, too true," the librarian said. "But may I say I think you're doing the right thing."

"Pardon me?" Bo replied, confused.

"I found a home, too, early on, in books. They saved me."

Bo looked at her, a large, round, resigned-looking being, surrounded on all sides by stacks of colorfully jacketed hard-covers. "Thanks," she said, "I appreciate that," and got out the door as quickly as she could.

She stopped on the steps and made two piles of the books she'd taken out. Then she pulled out the two plastic trash bags she'd tucked into her purse, deposited the books in them, trying to equalize the weight of each, and went to put them in the bicycle side baskets. But her bicycle was gone.

The worst thing about it, Bo thought as she trudged along carrying a plastic sack of books over each shoulder, was that she couldn't tell anybody. She couldn't tell her parents she'd managed to get her bike ripped off without telling them where and how. She wondered vaguely if Peter the sadist had helped himself to it. In any case, she certainly couldn't call the police. What if they asked why she was there in the first place?

Normally she'd confide in Weezie, but Weezie would never stand for this story. Bo could just hear her. "You pinhead, and just what were you intending to do with all this wonderful research material? Grind it up in the blender and feed it to Howard with a spoon?" Psychology soup, Bo thought to herself, and realized she was hungry. Well, why not? A five-mile ride and—how long had she walked now? —two miles at least. So there were three to go. She had just passed the sign that said Fairview—We Love Our Children and was headed down the main drag, such as it was. She had better call her mother and think of something convincing to tell her.

She found a phone at the Kentucky Fried Chicken and dialed home. "Oh, good," her mother said, assuming she was calling from the Parkview Library. "Did Louise find you? I sent her over there." Wonnnderful, Bo thought to herself. Well, she'd deal with it. Meanwhile she constructed something elaborate about meeting Darlene at the library and going home with her and not to try to phone there because they were expecting a long-distance call. "Fine," her mother said. "But remember, it's a school night. Ten-thirty at the latest." Bo checked her watch. Lying to her mother had made her even hungrier, but she only had an hour to go the three miles. She should just about manage it if she could keep a good pace. She hung up and started out, slinging the books over her shoulders again, catching sight of herself in the plate glass going out. She looked like Mrs. Santa Claus on the way to a funeral.

She slogged along, passing Dunkin Donuts, several boutiques, and a satellite-disk store, and found herself in the dark again. Fairview was a classier suburb than Kenview so it had fewer sidewalks, and she crossed to the other side of the road to be in view of oncoming traffic. The books were incredibly heavy. They'd better be worth it, she thought. They'd better tell me what I need to know. Then she wondered what she would do with the information.

She drew a fantasy in her head—not her usual fully fleshed-out sort, but a line drawing in the style of Peanuts.

She's sitting in a booth like Lucy with a sign: Psychiatric Help, 5 Cents. Howie appears wearing a sweater with a zigzag on it. "It's really very simple," she says to him and leans over and whispers. The books will have to fill in what she'll say. In the next frame he's skinny and walks off with a girl with naturally curly hair who looks an awful lot like Cyndy. She's left in the booth, with the books piled around her. The balloon reads, "What's wrong with this picture?"

Bo moaned out loud and shifted the left-hand sack to her right hand and vice versa. It didn't help. Her feet hurt horribly, and her whole body seemed to creak the way the bicycle had when she'd started out. She closed her eyes for a minute and trudged onward, just putting one foot in front of the other. She thought of the two of them, herself and Howard, at Mitch's right there in front of the whole world, eating together, and she felt better. She thought of sitting with him in the dark last week, the screen flickering in front of them, their hands occasionally meeting in the popcorn tub. Life was definitely better than it used to be. For her, anyway.

The going suddenly got tougher and she realized she'd encountered a hill. It was right at the top of it that a light suddenly flared and someone hit a horn. She jumped out of the way quickly, tripped on something, and toppled stomach-down into a ditch, sending both bags of books flying and knocking all the wind out of her.

In the same instant she heard brakes squeal, car doors bang, voices, and footsteps. She closed her eyes and thought she'd take a nap.

"Over here. It would have to be over here . . ." a man's voice called.

A woman's voice, high-pitched and anguished, but vaguely familiar, said, "We hit something. I know we did. It was big, and black. Could it have been a bear?"

"Don't be ridiculous. What would a bear be doing here? Here bear, here bear . . ." the man's voice called sarcastically.

"Richard, this isn't funny," the woman said. Bo knew she knew that voice from somewhere, but everything was fuzzy. "It could be lying half-dead around here . . ."

"What am I supposed to do, put it out of its misery? Sorry, I didn't bring a firearm."

"It could attack! It could be hurt and crazed and scared . . ." Yeah, Bo thought.

"Then why are we looking for it?" The man was beginning to sound impatient.

"Well, suppose it was a person? Suppose we hit a person, Richard."

"What sane person would wear black and walk along a suburban road at night?" he said. Bo wondered herself. "Anyway, this is Fairview. Nobody walks." Bo mustered all her strength and let out a sound, something between a moan and a squeak.

"Over there!" the woman's voice said, and she heard them moving toward her. With all her strength she managed to turn over and struggled to prop herself up on her elbows. When the light hit her face she had to close her eyes tight. "Oh my God . . ." the woman said. "Barbara?" Bo opened her eyes and could barely make out above the glare of a flashlight the face of Jan Albersham.

They sat at Kentucky Fried dunking nuggets into honey. "You were planning on walking all the way home to Parkview?" the man Ms. Albersham had introduced as Richard Sheridan asked her.

"I, uh, had trouble with my bike," Bo said. "I had to leave it."

"Couldn't you have called your folks?" he wondered. Bo had the sense he didn't believe her.

"Nobody home," Bo lied and stuck a nugget in her mouth.

"I still don't get why you went all the way to Kenview . . ." he started, but Ms. Albersham put a hand on his arm.

"For heaven's sake, Richard, let her be. She's wiped out, can't you see that?" He started to say something else, but Ms. Albersham picked up a nugget and fed it to him quickly. He looked surprised.

"Are you sure we shouldn't take you to a hospital for some X rays?" she asked Bo. "Nothing hurts?"

"I'm just kind of achy," Bo said. "But I'm sure nothing's broken. That's one good thing about all this padding." She smiled but Ms. Albersham didn't. "And I know I didn't hit my head. I landed on my stomach. And it definitely wasn't your fault," she added to Richard Sheridan. "I definitely tripped."

"In any case, I'm glad you weren't hurt. But you shouldn't have been walking out like . . ." He had to stop, finding that another nugget had been placed in his mouth.

Jan Albersham yawned. "She knows that, Richard."

"So," he said, after he had chewed and swallowed. "Tell us about your research. That looked like an interesting selection of titles." Bo had been mortified as they'd scoured the area for the books that had scattered: *Living and Dying, Fat and Thin, Winning the Losing Battle, Your Particular Grief* . . .

"Well, it's just a paper," she constructed quickly. ". . . I mean, two different papers . . . one for English and one for biology, sort of, um, aspects of grief expressed in literature . . ."

"That sounds ambitious," Sheridan said.

"And the other"—Bo was beginning to rather enjoy the inventing— "is about fat and your health. Mental health."

"That's very intelligent of you, Barbara," Ms. Albersham said. "It's a good way to start."

"Start?" Bo said, puzzled.

"Well, obviously the subject has relevance for you," Ms. Albersham said in the frank way she had that made Bo squirm. "And approaching it from the psychological angle makes sense."

"Gutsy, too," Sheridan said. Ms. Albersham looked at him and smiled. He looked pleased, as if she'd given him a gold star.

"Incidentally," Ms. Albersham said, "did you have *Fat Is a Feminist Issue* there? That's a marvelous book."

"No," Bo said. "They had it at the library, but I didn't get it because it didn't seem relevant." She meant relevant to Howard and his problem, of course, but there was no way for Ms. Albersham to know that. The teacher just looked at her oddly and said, "Well, we'd better get you home."

Bo walked in the door at ten-thirty on the dot. Her mother smiled the smile that said I-knew-I-could-count-on-you-baby.

12

A week later Bo sat on her bed surrounded by her research—eighty-seven three- by five-inch cards filled closely with her handwriting. She had sorted them into piles of what might apply to Howard's case and what was irrelevant. It irritated her that so much of the fat literature seemed devoted largely to the problems of females, with occasional thin chapters concerning fatness in males, as if maybe it didn't matter or men didn't care.

She had a lot more on fat than she did on grief, though. The death books depressed her, and she found them hard to read, even for Howard's sake. They seemed mostly to be about coping with long terminal illness, either in oneself or a loved one, rather than death that came fast and unwatched-for, as it had come for Howard's mother. She did have one card containing a brief, disturbing statement from a book by a minister addressing the reader's "traumatic grief" quite personally.

Your grief work will be longer, lonelier and more hazardous to your lasting emotional stability than if you had been able to anticipate the loss and converse with your loved one before death.

Oh right, she thought. It definitely would have helped if Mrs. Nevelson had mentioned to her son the fact that she was about to have a fatal accident. He could have gotten ready, then. Now, her own mother would have been more considerate and less spontaneous, Bo was sure. She had a sudden mad fantasy of Ruthanne's bringing up the subject:

"Bo-love, I'm really sorry but I'm going to have to pass away soon." (Bo was reasonably sure that even under such circumstances her mother would tend toward euphemism.) *"And I want you to know, baby, that it is absolutely, positively not your fault."*

"Which?" Bo said back to her shadowy mother.

Ruthanne looked at her wistfully and touched her hair. "Any of it, darling. Your weight. My life. The fact that your father is hardly ever home. That it took us ten years to conceive your sister after you were born. That she is thoroughly wonnnderful. That Howard got fat, too. You are NOT responsible."

"I know," Bo said loudly, wanting her fantasy to shut up now. But apparently the flimsy Ruthanne was on a roll.

"I mean it when I say it's not your fault about Howard, darling. After all, your fat didn't rub off on him, did it? And honestly, it's absolutely not your fault about the hijackings or any of the terrorist activities or apartheid or world hunger. Truly, darling!" Her mother's fantasy eyes were blazing now. *"It's not!"* She took Bo by the shoulders. *"Do you hear me? I'm proud of you!"* her mother said, frantically. *"Do you hear me? You have lovely skin and hair and eyes and such a pretty face and you're smart and sweet-tempered*

and good to your sister, and your father and I have always been so proud, so proud of you."

"You wouldn't be," Bo said suddenly to the wall. "You wouldn't be if you knew."

"Knew what?" Ruthanne shimmered a little. "Knew what, baby?"

"Who I am. How I am," Bo wanted to say, but it was hardly appropriate with her mother about to die. Instead she erased the last few moments of the fantasy and picked it up earlier.

"I'm proud of you," her mother said again. "And I wanted you to know that before I go."

"Ma, look, you don't have to," Bo said. "You really don't. Stay." But her mother wasn't listening.

"I just wanted you to know," Ruthanne repeated. "None of it is your fault."

The one thing Bo knew for sure was that in a crunch her mother could always be counted on to lie, just to make her feel better.

She picked up the cards again and thumbed through them. Several experts concurred that overeating sometimes had something to do with anger—that fat people were afraid of showing they were mad. That made sense to Bo, at least in terms of Howard. She herself, of course, didn't have a mad bone in her body, as Weezie often pointed out. But obviously, if your mother died like that it would make you angry, and it wasn't the kind of thing you could yell about openly. Eating over it seemed perfectly reasonable to Bo, and—she flipped through some cards in the grief pile and found one she remembered writing which confirmed that episodes of grief may in fact coincide with drastic increases in weight. Just as I suspected, she said to herself, feeling like Sherlock Holmes. Of course, it was going to be pretty hard to work all this into a conversation. Another theory she'd noted down was that some fat people were addicted to fatness rather than to overeating—that they ate just to stay fat. Bo frowned. That seemed dumb to her now. Why would you stay fat if you could be otherwise? The thing was, she didn't know what it was like to be thin, but Howard did, so why would he stay fat? She was sure, in fact, that he wasn't going to. Not if she had anything to say about it.

And then there was the problem of what would happen to their friendship once Howard was his old self again, but she couldn't afford to worry about that now. True love, her mother had told her often enough, involved giving till it hurt.

Howard wasn't exactly asking her to fix him, but she felt she owed him that much. Still, she'd have to be careful. One book cautioned that many fat people were given to depression when they tried to change their eating habits and lose weight. She knew that herself for a fact. And heaven knew Howard had had enough to be depressed about. She'd better take her time.

The last card she'd written said that the only "way out" of fatness was to learn to love one's fat personality while thinning. Well, if Howard couldn't love himself at the moment, at least she could do that much for him. She'd love him as much as he needed to be loved, and maybe, if she were lucky, she could keep him as a friend all her life.

13

On Columbus Day, a few weeks later, there was no school, and Howard had invited Bo over to help him and his father clean out their garage.

"Is this the stuff from which romance is made?" Bo had said to Weezie on the phone. Weezie kept insisting Howard's feelings for Bo were more than platonic, which Bo thought was dumb. She was reasonably sure he didn't have Cyndy over to clean out his garage. Why he did it, she thought, was to have her there as sort of a buffer between him and his father. She supposed his mother used to do that for them. It wasn't that the two of them fought. They didn't say much of anything, and when she was with them she noticed a lot of space between what anybody said. So maybe she wasn't a buffer. Maybe she was a filler. But as soon as she got there, she felt something in the air besides the dust they were raising.

"I say *out*," Howard was saying. Then there was a quiet space. The two of them were looking at a metal thing, a frame about six feet tall, like a rectangle set on its end, with some electronic-looking equipment in the middle. They didn't hear Bo come in; the garage door was open and she'd been walking on leaves.

"Well," George Nevelson said finally. "You never know."

"Yes you do." Bo thought Howard said this nicely but firmly. "*I* do. No way am I picking up on that project again." There was another quiet space.

"I understand that," his father said. "However, you could conceivably change your mind."

"No way," Howard said. Bo thought he looked edgy, as if in a minute his face would begin to get red or his breathing would get funny. "I'm too old for science fairs. I was already too old last year. It was a wacko idea to begin with. If everybody hadn't picked up on it so fast I'd've figured that out and never gotten this far." Bo still didn't know what they were talking about, but she had the feeling that "everybody" might have meant his mother. Maybe Cyndy, too.

There was another quiet space.

"Well," his father said in that long-drawn-out way Bo recognized. "It might come in handy."

Howard looked as though he would pop, but he didn't. He waited a moment, then said in a very careful voice, "What is anybody going to do with half an electron microscope?"

Bo took a breath and dived into the space. "You could have a garage sale." Her voice sounded enormous in there. They turned around, both of them looking surprised. "Hi," Bo said, feeling larger than life. Howard smiled at her. Did he look relieved? She thought she'd better keep it up, so she rattled off, "Yeah, you could do flyers: 'Big Deal Garage Sale—lawn furniture, sports equipment, kitchen stuff, electron microscope, old clothes and junk . . .'"

76

She wished right away that she hadn't said that about the old clothes, because she knew Howard's mother's things were still around. But Howard just kept smiling and said, "I wasn't sure you were going to show up."

"I came to help," Bo said, feeling dopey. Mr. Nevelson looked at Howard briefly, then gave Bo a weak smile and a nod.

"Good," Mr. Nevelson said. "You can mediate." So she wasn't supposed to buff or fill. She was supposed to mediate. It had a nice legal sound to it. "My thinking is, one day he'll decide he wants to finish it." George Nevelson waved at the giant microscope frame. Howard was behind him now and he rolled his eyes at Bo.

"Maybe," Bo said, in the best legal-sounding voice she could muster, "we should do the small stuff first. It piles up quicker that way and it feels more like you're getting something done."

Howard's father looked at her and smiled, a little half smile like the one that Howard had. "Very good," he said—she wasn't sure about what—and they all moved over to a pile of sports equipment in the corner.

Howard's father wasn't giving up, though. "Howard had a lot of publicity about that project," he said as they sorted through things. He made a head motion toward the microscope skeleton.

"I remember," Bo said, trying to sound noncommittal. She had in her own Howard collection an article the *Parkview Clarion* had run last fall: "Local Whiz Kid Will Do It Himself," telling all about how Howard was going to try something nobody had ever done on his own before—build an electron microscope from scratch.

Bo realized they were waiting in the silence, but she couldn't think of anything to add. She concentrated on the mess and tried to look industrious. Finally Howard said, "Dad, didn't you ever start something and not finish it?"

Bo held her breath. It seemed an incredibly nervy thing to say to a parent, especially to Mr. Nevelson, who had been trying to write a certain book for the last four years.

Howard's father didn't answer. He just sighed and said, "Okay, what about these ice skates?"

Afterward they went into the house for tea. Howard made real scones to go with it. Bo noticed that the living room was very neat. The mantel had only a couple of candlesticks on it. She wondered where all of Howard's trophies had gotten to—the ones his mother had collected and displayed there. Maybe he ate them.

When she thought about it walking home, the whole business scared her. It was as if Howard had been throwing pieces of himself away—the old self—the one she'd loved first. She'd had half an impulse to stop him, just as his father had wanted to, but she couldn't. She had to help him do what made him feel better. What were friends for?

The odd thing was that now she had exactly what she'd dreamed about: Howard was a regular fixture in her life. She didn't have to rewind her mental video or moon around about him. All she had to do was call him up. More usually, he called her. The fact that he looked like a version of himself done up for the Macy's Thanksgiving Day Parade was beside the point. Or was it?

The question is, Bo said to herself, did Howard suddenly start being my friend this year because I was—am— fat, or because of the show or my note to him or all of that stuff. I mean, suppose I'd gone on a diet this summer and come back to school thin and Howie had come back to school the way he is (say it, Butter, fat), *then* what would have happened? She saw the whole thing in a flash of fantasy. *He arrives at typing class, the way he did, a week and a half late. She's already in her seat wearing a soft blue sweater and designer jeans, in a size that comes from the Normal department. She spots him, registers what has happened to him, doesn't blink but says, "Hello, Howard, how are you?" They go to Mitch's and people see them together—fat him, thin her—applaud her courage, her generosity . . .*

Bo jerked her head up and stopped cold on the sidewalk. She felt sick at herself. Who do you think you *are*, Barbara Barrett. *Who?*

Who is Howie? her other self asked. That's all I'm trying to figure out. Who is Howie now? And what does he want with me?

14

It was toward the end of October that she began to notice the change in Reenie. Bo picked her up from ballet class and took her to buy new tights and leotards for her *Nutcracker* audition. The local ballet company did a Christmastime production using kids from the various dance studios in the area. Reenie'd been mad to do it ever since she'd heard, even though she'd only taken lessons for a year.

"What's wrong with your old tights?" Bo asked her.

"They're old," Reenie replied with her isn't-it-obvious look.

A star is born, Bo thought and led her sister into the specialty store, one of those tiny places with everything in boxes or behind a counter, where you always had to ask. Bo felt as though she filled up the whole space between the counter and the wall. There was only one salesclerk, who had her back turned when they walked in. A little bell rang when they opened and closed the door, but the woman behind the counter didn't turn around. Finally Bo said, "Um, a leotard and tights?'' The woman turned and looked at her, and her eyebrows shot up under her bangs, which were dyed red. Bo let her wonder for a minute and then nodded toward Reenie saying, "For her." The saleslady hadn't even seen Reenie because she was shorter than the counter. The woman looked relieved, and smiled the isn't-she-adorable smile most people still gave to Reenie. "Small, of course," the saleslady said.

Reenie didn't smile back. Instead she said in a loud mean voice, "No. Medium."

"Oh, I don't think so, baby," the woman said.

"I'm not a baby," Reenie said in the same loud voice. Bo put her hand on her sister's shoulder, but Reenie jerked herself away.

The woman's eyebrows disappeared again. She turned around and checked the stock and brought down two boxes. Without saying anything she opened both of them and took out two leotards, flipping each one of them over the counter. "Small," she said, patting one with her hand, and, "Medium," patting the other, which was much bigger. Then she looked Reenie straight in the face and said, "Did you want to see the large?"

Reenie didn't flinch. She just pointed to the medium and said, "We'll take this one." Then she turned around to examine a rack of socks, which gave Bo the chance to signal the woman to wrap up the small leotard and tights to go with it. The woman looked disapproving but did it. Bo paid and was handed the package. "They shouldn't be spoiled at this age," the saleslady said. "Especially the pretty ones."

"Thank you," Bo said and left. She figured she'd get the things home and cut out the labels or something. She knew she shouldn't let Reenie get away with that behavior, but she didn't have time to deal with it, either. Howard was picking her up at two. She supposed that was part of Reenie's problem these days—Bo didn't have as much time or inclination to be her best pal. Or maybe she was just plain jealous.

Well, that was okay. In fact, it was kind of a nice change. The thought made Bo feel guilty, but she rather enjoyed it.

They walked home in silence. "Can I have it?" Reenie asked, nodding to the package when they got there.

"I'll, uh, wash them out for you, okay? You shouldn't wear things right from the store." Her sister shrugged and started upstairs but turned back.

"Butter?" Reenie had adopted their mother's phony-casual look. "If I make the *Nutcracker* will you come to all the performances?"

Bo wanted to hug her but thought maybe it wasn't the time. "Sure, lovebug," she said. "I'll try."

Reenie looked even more casual. "Will you bring Howard?"

"Sure," Bo said. "At least I'll ask him."

"Good," Reenie said and went upstairs.

Two days before Halloween, when Howard asked Reenie what she was going to be and she said a ghost, Bo could have kicked her.

"I thought you were going to be a ballet dancer."

"Not for Halloween," Reenie replied in a voice she used a lot lately, as if Bo were the dumbest person in the world. "I'm going to be a dancer, *really*, so why would I dress up and pretend to be one?"

"Her logic is unassailable, as usual," Howard said and winked, Bo wasn't sure if at her or Reenie.

"All I know is Ma's going to be disappointed." Reenie looked stricken and Bo felt mean but satisfied. That child got her so mad lately.

"Disappointed how?" Howard asked.

"Because Ma loves to sit up half the night before Halloween making a big deal fancy costume. I made her miserable one year when I asked to have a 'bought' costume from the dime store like most of the other kids had."

"Did you get it?" Howard asked.

"I would have. Ma used to hate to disappoint me. But we couldn't get one to fit. Of course when Ma made *me* a costume I was usually something cute and fat like a pumpkin or a chipmunk. I'd've given my eyeteeth to be a ballet dancer. I hate to say it, but sometimes I think some people are a little spoiled."

Reenie wasn't troubled. "Annnyway," she said, grabbing Howard's arm and pulling it around him. "I'm making my own costume. I guess Ma can help if she needs to." Howard pretended he was caught, struggled free, and allowed her to catch him again. "I'm just gonna get an old white pillowcase . . ." She pinned both of Howard's arms behind him.

"I hate to tell you, sugar," Bo said, although she didn't really, "but we don't have any old white pillowcases in this household. There's nothing but flowers or stripes or beige or blue or Sesame Street." Reenie looked stricken again and set Howard free.

"I'll take a look over at my house," he said. Bo could have bopped him. "My mother thought colored sheets were decadent. No offense meant," he offered Bo, who carefully looked as if she didn't care. "I don't guarantee they're very white, though. She was a crummy housekeeper. Always said we had the kind of wash somebody on television would be ashamed of."

Reenie was walking around the room, her arms extended, practicing spook noises. "*Whooo . . . Whooo . . .*" She came up behind Howard and tried to climb up his back. He reached back and made a sling with his arms. She tried to step into it but kept missing. Bo felt a chill and went upstairs to get a sweater.

When she came back Reenie was on Howard's shoulders, still doing her ghost act. "*Whooo . . . Whooo . . .*"

"You're getting good," he said, whirling her around.

"Is that really what ghosts do?" Reenie asked as he put her down.

"Hey, Reen . . ." Bo started, sensing danger.

"I'm no expert," Howard said. "But that's what I always heard."

"Butter said your mother died."

"That's true," Howard said, no change on his face.

"Reen," Bo said quickly, "would you go get my pencil case, just 'cause I'm lazy. I left it on my desk upstairs."

"I don't feel like it," Reenie said, still intent on Howard. "Is your mother a ghost now?" she asked, really wondering.

"Cooky, I really need it," Bo said, feeling desperate.

"There are pencils down here. Over there," Reenie said, pointing, and asked again. "Is she—a ghost—your mother?"

Howard had been thinking about it and said, "I see her around now and then."

Annoyed as she was at her sister, Bo now raced to protect her, saying, "Howard, she's so little. *I* know what you mean but you might confuse her."

Reenie was relentless. "Where do you see your mother, Howie? What does she look like?"

"Reenie . . ." Bo raced back to Howard's side. He interrupted.

"Listen, kiddo, your sister's right," he said, giving Reenie a nice smile. "I was talking through my hat. Dead's dead."

Bo raced back again on behalf of the small one now, and said through her teeth, "You're going to scare her, Howard."

Reenie, who had very good ears, said, "I'm not scared. I just never knew anybody dead before. They don't really wear sheets, do they?"

"No," Howard said. "That's sort of poetic license."

"When they put them in the ground," Reenie started

thoughtfully—Bo was shaking by now—"is it like planting? Do they grow back?"

"No," Howard said, but his voice was beginning to sound a little hollow.

"If my mother dies I hope she comes back like that," Reenie said.

"Reenie," Bo said, exhausted from trying to protect them both, "Ma isn't going to die."

"Sure she is," Reenie said, matter-of-factly. "Everybody does. It was Mama who told me. Not till they're old, though. Was your mother very old?" She addressed Howard again.

"Not as old as you're supposed to be," he answered.

"How come?"

"Somebody slipped up, I guess," Howard offered. It was clear this wasn't a new thought to him.

"Who?" Reenie asked. "God?"

Howard thought a minute and shrugged. "Nobody's perfect," he said.

Bo was shocked speechless for a moment. "Hey, Reen," she finally managed, "why don't you go and get yourself a Creamsicle. I saw Ma got some when she shopped yesterday."

Reenie ran off. Howard called out to her, "Would you get me one, too?"

"Yeah," Bo called to her sister. "Get us all one."

15

Weezie had started to act weird, too. One morning on the way to school Bo had mentioned that Palmer had been out the day before and they'd had a substitute again. "Palmer gets the 'flu' a lot," she said. "Almost always on a Monday. I wish she'd get some help for her problem." She had meant this sincerely. Weezie got her mean look on, which of course was nothing new, but Bo didn't expect her to say what she said.

"Well," she started, "everybody's got something, don't they? I mean, Palmer's into booze, my mom's into bridge, your dad's into work, work, work . . ." Bo was shocked but Weezie went right on like a song, "Marvin's into wisecracks, Tiger's into turtles, Howard's into food, you're into Howard . . ."

"Excuse me, Louise," Bo stopped her. "What exactly are you saying?"

"That everybody's some kind of addict or other. Everybody's got the munchies for something—or somebody. It's a sick world." And she walked away.

A few days later they'd been at Mitch's. They'd both had projects after school, so by the time they got there the place was nearly empty, which was fine with Bo. "It's not that I still don't like our crowd, at least individually, most of them, but they seem, I don't know, younger than they used to." Weezie glared. "I didn't mean you, dope," Bo said and smiled.

"No?"

"No," Bo said and stopped smiling.

They were nursing Tabs. After a minute Weezie said, "You're eating less, aren't you?"

It sounded to Bo like an accusation. "Sometimes," she said, not wanting to commit herself. "Just as an example. To get him started."

Louise swore quietly.

"What's wrong with that?" Bo asked. She really wondered.

Weezie was hitting her head with the flats of her hands. "I wouldn't mind . . . I wouldn't mind if you were trying to lose weight *because* of Howard. But *you* are trying to lose weight *for* Howard."

"You're making an awful lot of a preposition," Bo replied.

"It's true!" Weezie looked fierce. "Tell me I'm wrong. You just admitted it. You're not trying to make yourself pretty because you love him and want him. That would be normal. Revolting, but normal. *You* are trying to set an example so Howard dear will pick up on it, lose weight, go back to being the prince of Parkview High School, and walk off into the sunset with Cyndy spelled with two Y's!"

Bo stared at her empty glass and poked the piece of lemon at the bottom with a straw.

"AM I WRONG???" Weezie was almost yelling.

"Something like that," Bo admitted. "So?"

"SO. It's sick!" Weezie threw two quarters on the table and banged out.

Bo fished the piece of lemon out of the Tab with her straw and sucked at it. It was lonely having Louise disapprove of her.

What Weezie had said about her dad in passing had stuck with Bo, and one night when it was after eight and he hadn't gotten home yet, she tried to edge into the subject with her mother. They were drying dishes. Her father's dinner sat on the kitchen counter covered with Saran Wrap, waiting to have warmth restored to it by the microwave. Ruthanne, who had used a lot of pots and pans in the preparation, was banging them around a bit.

"Is there such a thing as a workaholic?" Bo said to her mother.

Her mother checked the clock out of the corner of her eye. "What makes you ask?" she said. Bo knew from her voice that she knew why she was asking.

"Oh, I don't know," Bo said. "There's everything else." She grabbed a handful of chow mein noodles from a dish, also waiting for her dad. She'd fallen off the food wagon again. Anyway, she was sure Howard wasn't ready. "I mean," she said with her mouth full, "there are all kinds of addictions."

"Did someone use that term to you specifically?" Ruthanne asked. She frowned at the bottom of a pot and got out the copper cleaner.

"No, I sort of made it up and then I realized I'd heard it before."

"Where was that?" Her mother rubbed at the pot, quite hard.

Bo decided to skip the games. "Is Daddy one?"

Strangely enough, Ruthanne decided to skip the games, too. She looked up at the ceiling. They could hear Reenie stomping around up there and the occasional clatter of dropped wooden blocks. "Butter, I don't know," her mother said. "Sometimes I wonder. He likes to work. He needs to work. He makes us money. We don't go without."

"Without what?" Bo said, not sure what she meant.

"Life's essentials . . . home . . . food . . . a decent standard of living. Your father works hard for these things. I've never wanted a career, but I'd be happy to get a part-time job, at least when Irene's a little older, but he won't hear of it. Even when he's home he's busy doing things on the house. For us. You can't complain because someone is industrious."

Bo looked thoughtful. "I suppose," she said, taking more noodles, "there can be too much of a good thing?"

"Would you like me to heat up some more chow mein, darling, if you didn't have enough? There's plenty left," her mother offered.

"No thanks. I mean . . ." Bo said, trying hard to stick to her point, though it scared her, "sometimes people do things and do them because they don't want to do something else. Like, okay, I'm fat because I always was and I eat because I always did. But with Howard it's different. He was perfectly normal. He was fantastic. Then his mother died and it did something. I think he eats to fill up the big hole inside him. He's unhappy and it hurts too much."

"Has he told you that?" her mother asked.

"Of course he hasn't. He can't. That's the point!"

"You don't have to be rude," Ruthanne said, and banged the now shiny pot down. "I'm listening. You're saying that Howard eats because he can't face his grief." Her voice had thinned out a little. "That's possibly so. That's very sensitive of you. But you began by discussing your father. Are you saying he works hard because he's unhappy? Is that what you're suggesting?"

Bo backed off. "I'm not suggesting anything, Ma," she

said. "What do I know? It's just I've been noticing that sometimes people kind of get hooked on one thing or another. That's all."

"I'm sure that's so," her mother allowed. "And possibly your father is 'hooked,' so to speak, on working. But he's happy when he does it. That much I'm sure of. When he works around this house, he whistles, for heaven's sake. You don't whistle if you're unhappy." Where is that written? Bo wondered, but didn't say so.

"I like to cook," her mother went on, her voice a little higher. "I cook a great deal. Is there something odd about that? Just because you enjoy doing something doesn't mean you're a candidate for the analyst's couch. You yourself said you enjoy eating a great deal, right?" Bo's cheeks were too full of noodles to reply; she nodded. "Are you unhappy?" her mother asked. She had picked up a large iron frying pan.

Bo chewed for a moment, swallowed, and finally said, "Actually, I've never been happier."

"I thought so," Ruthanne said triumphantly. She tore off a paper towel and wiped the bottom of the pan. "When you are unhappy I generally know about it. If you were, I'd feel terrible."

The following week Ms. Palmer was fired for showing up at school too drunk to teach. Everyone was talking. Bo was depressed by the gossip and said as much to Ms. Albersham as they were sorting submissions to *The Vigil*. (Bo still hadn't said yes to the editor's job, but Ms. Albersham was holding it open.) She was surprised by her teacher's hard-line response.

"Best thing that could happen to her," she said.

"You really think?" Bo said, and searched Ms. Albersham's face for compassion. It was there, but it wasn't uppermost. Ms. Albersham nodded, looking serious.

"I do think. Definitely."

Bo was amazed and uncomfortable. Ms. Albersham had always seemed to her the soul of tolerance.

"Sometimes," her teacher went on, "people with problems have to bottom-out before they smarten up."

"But isn't she sick?" Bo said. "Isn't alcoholism a disease? I bet she has a hard life we don't even know about. I bet that's why . . ."

"Honey, *why* isn't the point. *What is* is the point. We can understand and commiserate till we're blue in the face, but that isn't going to help her."

"What will help her, then?" Bo asked. She suddenly felt she had a stake in the situation. "I mean they ought to be able to do something."

"They?" Ms. Albersham raised an eyebrow.

"Well, whoever . . ." Bo started. "Whoever she has. She must have people who care about her—who love her. Or doesn't she? Is that why?"

"As a matter of fact, Edith Palmer has a sister named Eloise who's been loving her to death. Maybe she's finally smartened up. For years she's been protecting and enabling and—Jan, what are you doing?—I'm sorry, Barbara, I've said too much. This really isn't appropriate . . ." Ms. Albersham looked upset with herself.

"Oh, please, don't stop now," Bo said quickly. "Don't pull rank on me . . ." She put a hand to her mouth, stunned at her own boldness. "I mean . . . this could be important."

"I'm sorry." Ms. Albersham sighed. "Do you have . . . is there someone with an alcohol problem close to you?"

"No," Bo said, "not alcohol. But there are other kinds of things—like food."

"Ah," Ms. Albersham said and looked pleased. "So you really are facing up. I thought the research would help."

"It wasn't for me," Bo confessed. "It was for a friend."

Ms. Albersham laughed. "Do you know how many

people call Alcoholics Anonymous for help saying it's for a friend? You can drop that pretense."

"But it really is," Bo said. "It really is for a friend."

"I see," Ms. Albersham said. "That would be the boy I see you with now and then."

"Howard," Bo whispered.

"Oh my dear." Her teacher sighed. "You really do have a problem."

"Howard's is worse," Bo said resolutely.

"No, Barbara," Ms. Albersham said. The compassion was now right on top. "Yours is worse because you think Howard's is."

16

The day after Thanksgiving Bo and Howard sat at her kitchen table picking over the leftovers, a large turkey carcass between them. Howard applied a knife to what was left on the bones on one side. He would carve a thin slice and lay it lovingly in the flat plastic container provided by Ruthanne. On the other side Bo hacked away with a dull paring knife, or pulled at the remaining meat with her fingers, handing Howie a piece to nibble and popping one into her mouth. About every third piece landed in the Tupperware.

"Your mother was crazy to ask us to do this," Howard said with a grim little smile.

"She's trying to establish trust," Bo said with her mouth full. "Listen, we're doing everybody a favor. If we didn't take the meat off the bones she'd put the whole thing in this huge pot and make soup."

"So?" Howard said, chewing.

"I don't really like soup," Bo explained. "There's nothing to chew."

"True," Howard said. "Cream soup's okay, though."

"Cream soup's the best," Bo said. "Or soup with a lot of stuff in it. The kind you can grate cheese all over."

"Ever have cold soup?" Howard asked. He studied the bird a moment, wondering how to get at the rest. "My mother used to . . ." He stopped.

"Go on," Bo said, carefully watching the turkey. She tried to encourage him on the subject, but not make an issue of it. Grief, all the books said, had its own timetable and its own set of steps. As nearly as she could tell, Howard was still in the denial stage, despite what he'd said to Reenie about dead's being dead.

Howard started to saw at the meat again. "She used to make all sorts of neat cold soups in the summertime. Cucumber . . . let's see . . . borscht? That's beets with sour cream in globs in it. . . . Carrot soup?" Bo made a face. "No, really. She made this neat soup out of carrots all mushed up that could be either hot or cold. A lot of cream in it either way." He licked his lips. "And nutmeg, I think. I tried to make it last summer when I was learning to cook, but it turned out like baby food."

"Yuk," Bo said, but pain for him tugged at her as usual: the notion of Howard alone in the kitchen, going through a recipe file, the cards written in his mother's writing. How long would it take for him to understand down deep that even if he made every recipe in the file and ate it up, again and again, she wasn't coming back?

"I'll try it again sometime," he said of the soup. "You might like it."

"Don't do me no favors, kid," Bo growled.

"Got to be a first time for everything," Howard said. "Got to try new things." Bo would have said, "Says who?" but she knew it had probably been Mrs. Nevelson. Instead she handed him another piece of turkey. She felt a vague stab of jealousy in her heart and dismissed it as idiotic.

"I guess I'm just not into carrots," she said. "They remind me of diets. Speaking of which, my friend . . ."

"Not now!" Howard said and pointed the carving knife right at her. She jumped back and raised her hands in mock surrender.

"Okay, okay, but we did say . . ."

"After the holidays." He removed the final piece of meat, looked at it a moment and ate it. "Maybe," he added.

"That's a month," Bo protested, but her heart wasn't in it. So far she'd failed consistently in the subtle guidance department. Maybe she should try not-so-subtle.

"Actually," she began tentatively, "I've been reading up on it."

"On?" He gave her his whatever-do-you-mean look.

"Obesity," she clarified. His face didn't change. "As in fat?"

Howard shrugged. "Whatever turns you on," he said and gave her a grin she regarded as phony.

"Don't get mad at me . . ." she said.

"I don't get mad much," he reassured her. She knew it was so. Just like the books said. It was another thing they had in common, but she worried about it in his case. It was different for a man. "Where is that written?" someone said in her head. It sounded like Jan Albersham.

"Don't get mad," she repeated, "but are you at all aware of the dire things fat can do to you?"

"I bet I will be in a minute," he said. He had begun to look tired.

She took a deep breath. "Fat can contribute to diabetes, arthritis, high blood pressure, varicose veins, kidney disease, constipation, inflammation of the gallbladder, and problems during pregnancy and childbirth," she rattled off, amazed she had memorized this.

"I'll bear that in mind," he said, with an edge she wasn't accustomed to hearing. "Especially the last."

"Howard, I'm not trying to be pushy . . ." she began.

"You could have fooled me," he said back, stopping her in her tracks. His face still looked nice enough but his tone of voice scared her half to death. She saw him in her mind carefully washing the turkey grease off his hands like a surgeon and walking out of her life forever.

"It's just that," she tried to explain, "I know *I* need to do something about my weight and I thought maybe we could do it together."

"Maybe we can," he allowed. "Sometime." Obviously the time was going to be up to him. Well, at least she'd have him in her life a while longer. There was that.

"So," he said, in the nature of a punctuation mark, "what do we do with him now?" Bo wondered if he meant himself, but then saw he was looking down at the turkey's bare bones.

She made a playing-dumb face at him. "I don't know. Shine him up? Sand him down? Make an art object out of him?" Bo offered. "We throw him out, nitwit."

"Out here?" Howie picked up the carcass in both hands and made as if to pitch it out the window.

"Right," Bo said, grinning and opening a drawer to look for trash bags. "Open this, would you?" she said, handing one to Howard.

"*Me* open it? Why me? Sneaking sexism around here. Next thing you'll be asking me to take the garbage out."

"Because I'm all greasy and it keeps slipping around." Bo showed him her hands.

"I'm as greasy as you are."

"Nyah nyah nyah," Bo said and made a face.

"You sound like your sister."

"Too bad I don't look like her."

"I don't know. She's very short."

Giggling, Bo finally succeeded in getting the bag opened.

"Toss," she said. He tossed the carcass in. "Poor Tom, not even a decent burial," she said, and could have kicked herself for it. But it didn't seem to bother Howard. He tied the top of the bag around itself and went out the back door. She heard the lid of the trash can bang hard.

17

The first week in December Howard's Aunt Marcia came to visit. She had expected Howard and his father in Syosset for Thanksgiving, but at the last minute an icy snow had turned the roads too slick for driving, and it was too late to get reservations on the holiday-crowded airways. There had been several dutiful invitations from friends and colleagues, Bo's mother included, but George and Howard had decided to skip the whole thing and go Chinese.

Marcia was wild when she heard. She sat in Marion Nevelson's chair, a tote bag advertising public television at her feet. "Shrimp with black bean sauce! Don't you see that's *avoidance*?"

Howard excused himself and went upstairs to do his homework, and to give her the chance to talk about him. She hadn't seen him since midsummer, when he was still edging outward from pudgy, and she hadn't been able to control her face when they'd picked her up at the airport. He was, of course, used to the look people gave to the change in him, but to have it come across features so like his mother's had disarmed him.

When his mother was alive he had found comparing the two of them interesting, from a scientific point of view. He had wondered about the isolated gene that carried the swirl of yellow hair at the nape of each of their necks, though Marcia wore her long hair either skinned back in a pony tail or pinned up every which way, while his mother's was always cut short and sometimes professionally curled.

The two of them had variations on the same voice, too, although where his mother's had been rich and full, Marcia's had an Eastern sharpness that now penetrated the uncarpeted area of his room. Without trying to he heard words like *compensation* and *alienation* and *acting out*. He couldn't make out his father's responses. Finally he put on a record.

A little while later she knocked on the door. "Howie? May I invade your space?" How do you answer a question like that, he wondered, so he didn't. She came in. "Your dad has asked me to go through her things. I don't know if I can handle it by myself. Do you think? . . ." Instead of finishing her question she made a pained but hopeful face. Although Howard knew almost immediately that his father had asked no such thing, he followed her into the master bedroom.

Forty minutes later there were piles of clothing, shoes, personal odds and ends all over the room. Marcia's object, apparently, was to draw him out. He felt a mixture of resentment and sympathy toward his father for letting her try, knowing it was probably the blond swirl and the like voice that convinced him.

"I'm worried about your dad," was the first thing she said. "He says so little about her. Keeps everything bottled up. That's a time bomb, you know?" She was going through a tangle of scarves, pulling each one out long and laying it lengthwise on the bed. ". . . The one thing I've learned in umpteen years of therapy, if nothing else, is you've got to feel your feelings.''

Howard had a flashback of his mother the first time she'd heard this phrase, a letter of Marcia's on brown recycled-paper stationery dangling in her hands. They'd all called her Aunt Marshmallow back then. His mother was honestly mystified. "Feel your feelings?" he remembered her saying. "What on earth else would you do with them?"

Now, Howard said nothing and started to sort earrings, carefully keeping his back to Marcia, who was examining a pile of underthings. "I have such a sense of her this minute," she went on. "Not just her things, but the idea of her. And sometimes I feel so helpless and so, I don't know, so angry. As if I could change it if I just tried hard enough. Then I know that's not so. That's when I get mad. Do you ever feel angry about it?" she said, an edge of hopefulness in her voice.

Howard felt weary. He sifted out the mate of an amethyst earring and lined up the two of them. "Yeah," he said. "I guess so." Marcia looked unconvinced.

"I get mad, too, when I think about her and what she didn't do for herself. She had such incredible potential. But my sister just wasn't into self-actualization."

Howard took another handful out of the chaotic jewelry box and sifted through it with his fingers, adding to the pairs of earrings on the dresser. He was left with a blue glass pin with a bent fastener, and several small, hard, odd-shaped white objects. At first he couldn't figure out what they were. After a moment he recognized them as his baby teeth.

He set them down abruptly and surveyed the room. "We need some boxes, right?" he said, and headed out. Aunt Marshmallow looked after him and bit her lip.

He stopped on the way back from the basement and called Bo, just to ask her how Gibson was doing. She was boarding him for the weekend because he made Marcia wheeze. Something in his voice—a careful flatness—made Bo wonder if he needed her. "Are you doing anything important?" she asked.

"No," he said in such a way that she was certain.

"I thought I might stop by," she said. "My geometry's giving me fits. Maybe you could straighten me out on some principles?"

She appeared ten minutes later. Marcia answered the door and took in a sharp breath at her silhouette—an adolescent mountain outlined against the arc of the streetlight, carrying a shining aluminum foil package that turned out to be pumpkin bread.

18

"**I** will. I really will, first thing. It's just it's hard to plan. We both have these obligations, you know? See you." Bo hung up the phone and went back to the kitchen table where Howard had just poured her a Tab. "Annette," she said and sighed. "She keeps wanting to double-date with us." She gave the word *double-date* quotation marks with her hands.

"So what'd you say?"

"I hedged. For the ninety-ninth time. Weeze says she just wants to be seen with you. I'm her link to greatness." Howard gave a little snort. "Well, she is a climber. But she can't help it. And I hate to keep hurting her feelings."

"How come you never ask me if I want to go out with them?"

"You don't," Bo said. "You'd hate Marvin. He's an adolescent infant. I mean, God knows he's got his reasons. He's got an older brother who's a giant brain at M.I.T. And sisters who are twelve and twins. And all Marvin can think of to be is asinine."

"I guess ya works with what ya got," Howard said.

"But he is hard to take." Bo shuddered a little.

"And you're protecting me," Howard added.

"I am not," Bo said, not sure exactly what she was doing. "I'm protecting us."

"Aha," Howard said, tipping back in his chair.

"Besides its being a big bore," she explained, "if we're seen with them people could get the wrong idea about us, you know?"

"What idea is that?" he said, looking at her blankly. She hated his playing dumb.

"That we're a . . . an item or something."

"God forbid. The blubber couple." She gave him a pained look. "That was supposed to be funny," he added.

"It was," she said and smiled. "But let's keep it an inside joke, okay? Anyway, I told her we don't date, as such. We just go out together sometimes."

He looked even blanker. "Did she grasp the distinction?"

"I don't know. She has kind of a small mind."

Howard sipped his Tab briefly. "How good a friend is Annette?"

Bo was annoyed. "On a scale of one to ten?"

"I mean it."

"How *good* a friend is she or how good a *friend* is she?" Bo asked.

"Why do I put up with this woman?" Howard said and looked at her fondly in a way that confused her.

"I don't know if I can call her a friend at all," Bo said, thinking about it. "It's just, I've known her forever. Would you believe we were Brownies together?"

"Chocolate or butterscotch?"

"Give me a break, will you? Brownies are what you are before you're Girl Scouts. Except Annette never was a Girl Scout."

"How come?" Howard said, his mouth now full of ice. "They bar sexpots?"

Bo felt a little brittle. He looked at her blandly and waited for her reply.

"She lost interest, I guess. So did I, to tell you the truth, but my mother was the troop leader. It was fly up or out. Fly up is what you do to get from being a Brownie to a Scout."

"Girls lead complex lives, don't they?" he said, crunching ice.

"You weren't a Scout?"

"Nope. My mother thought they were repressive."

Bo grinned. "I'd've liked your mother."

"She'd've liked you." There was a brief silence. Something raced inside of Bo that she couldn't catch. Finally she said casually, "Do you really think Annette's sexy?"

"Did I say that?" Howard asked. "Think, now."

"You implied it."

"No, *you* inferred it."

Bo grinned, adoring him for knowing the difference.

"No," he went on. "I don't think she's sexy. I think she thinks she's sexy."

"She's got a nice figure," Bo said generously.

"It's pointed, for Pete's sake. They ought to ship her to the Pentagon as a secret weapon." Bo, who was in the middle of gulping her Tab, gave a laugh that made bubbles in it. "Okay," Howard said. "Now tell me the poor, sad, sociological reasons Annette Morisi is driven to wearing a pair of funnels for a bra." Bo laughed so hard into the glass it almost tipped. She righted it quickly.

"I don't know," she said, getting herself together. "To ward off Marvin?"

"I see. I see. She gives him these come-hither glances, but when he comes hither—whammo—stainless steel. Maybe we *should* go out with them. I'll slip him a can opener."

Bo blushed. "Stop it. I'm beginning to feel guilty," she said.

"For?" he queried.

"For saying rotten things about my friends."

"Eat something," he suggested and passed her the potato chips.

Marvin opened the door to his father's car, reached in and pulled up the back door lock. "Drive, would you, Nevelson?" he said, tossing Howard the keys. Before Howard could answer Marvin had opened the back door and given Annette a push in the vicinity of her behind.

Howard saluted him and then bowed low to Bo as she got in the front seat. "Thank-kew, James," she said, and he moved around to the driver's seat.

"What're you, Sir Galahad?" Marvin said from the rear. "Take it from me, they do better with a push in the tush." Howard ignored this and closed the car door, plunging them all into total darkness. There was a new inch of snow on the windshield. Marvin made a low appreciative sound. "Hey, why don't we stay right here?"

"And they'll find our frozen bodies in the morning," Bo said.

" 'Teenagers Die After the Ballet.' Be rotten for the box office," Marvin said. "Somebody better scrape. There's only one scraper."

"Toss you?" Howard offered.

Marvin coughed. "Well, I took care of it on the other end. It snowed all afternoon, remember?" He looked to Annette and winked since she'd been at his place when his mother brought the car back from the mall, nicely thawed out.

"Right," Howard said and started the motor so the defroster would begin to work at the window.

Bo sat rigid, looking forward into the blade of Howard's scraper. There was a thin film of ice under the snow. In the backseat an extreme silence was broken suddenly by Annette squealing, "Not *now*." Howard was scraping a round circle directly in front of Bo. When he had cleared it he peered inside at her and made a ridiculous face. She made one back and started out of the car.

"Where are you going?" Marvin said.

"To help him, of course."

"With what?"

"My bare hands," she said and started to close the door.

"Wait a minute," Marvin said. "Use this." He handed her his father's Amoco credit card.

"So," Marvin said when they were on their way. "What'd you think of the belly dance?"

"It was beautiful," Annette said. "I've always wanted to see the *Nutcracker Suite*."

"It was the whole *Nutcracker*," Howard corrected her politely. "The *Nutcracker Suite*'s what you get on a record. This was the whole thing." Bo felt absurdly proud of him. In the backseat, Annette looked impressed.

"If you ask me," Marvin said, though nobody had, "those guys wear padded jockstraps."

"Is that what you did all night, Newton?" Howard said amiably. "Watch crotches?" Annette giggled and Bo squirmed.

"So? I never saw a real live ballet before. Had to take in all the sights. You know, it's the girls that ought to wear the falsies, though. There wasn't a decent pair in the whole bunch."

"Your sister was adorable, Butter," Annette said, breaking the silence that followed. "Does she want to be a dancer when she grows up?"

"Don't we all?" Bo said. Howard looked over at her and smiled. She felt better.

"Tell her the pay's lousy," Marvin said. "They can't even sell all the tickets. Not that I didn't appreciate the freebies, Butterball."

"I did when I was little," Annette said, a little dreamily. "Want to be a dancer, I mean. I took toe and tap and baton twirling from the time I was four."

" 'On the good ship Lollipop . . .' " Marvin sang and did a soft shoe with his hands. Howard glanced at Bo to see how she was holding up.

"I remember you used to dance," she said to Annette. "What happened?"

"I don't know," Annette said. "I got tired, I guess."

"I'll bet," Howard said. Annette smiled at the back of his head.

" 'You never smile, Annette-Marie,' my mother used to go. 'You've got to have a big smile.' My first recital. I'm this little kid, right? Working my tail off, wearing this little black jobby—sequined lapels and a little top hat with glitter all over it? 'Smile, Annette,' she goes. 'People will think you don't *like* to dance.' "

"I don't know," Howard said. "But if I was four years old and doing toe and tap and baton twirling I wouldn't smile much, either."

Bo glanced back at Annette who was looking at Howard appreciatively. Marvin looked miffed. "Anyway"—Annette sighed—"I did it for eight more years and then I guess I figured there must be more to life."

"Like men," Marvin offered and blew in her ear. Annette giggled and put her head on his shoulder. "Anyway, I thought it was gorgeous. I love it when the tree grows. It makes me feel like a kid again."

"Awww," Marvin said, but she ignored him.

"What did you like best, Butter?"

"Outside of my sister?" Bo said. "The 'Waltz of the Flowers.' I know it's corny but I love it."

"Hey, I liked that number, too," Marvin said, surprising them all. "Only I was hoping they were gonna peel the petals. How about you, How? Don't you think a little strip woulda livened things up? Not that you coulda told the girls from the boys with their clothes off . . ."

"What did you like best, Howard?" Bo said, quite loudly.

"Me? I liked the whole thing."

Marvin whistled in mock admiration. "The boy's a regular culture vulture."

"I like the Russian number and the Arabian thing . . ."

"Well, now, *there*," Marvin started, but Howard continued over him.

"And I like the bit where the two of them are dancing and the snow starts coming down. Nice effect."

Bo glowed. "The snow pas de deux! That's my favorite, too. That and the flowers."

"Patty-who?" Marvin said. "Pardon me. I no speaka da ballet."

"Pas de deux," Annette said importantly, "means a dance for two. Remember when the Snow King and Queen— the ones in white—danced together and then it snowed? I mean, it was so romantic."

"Oh, yeah, I remember. Which one was the queen?" Marvin said and laughed hysterically.

In the front seat Bo sighed and Howard switched on the radio.

The fine snow had turned to large lazy flakes. Howard turned the windshield wiper to slow and maneuvered the radio dial. "What the devil is that?" Marvin called from the backseat."

"FM," Howard answered.

Marvin started to say something but apparently was

stopped. "Did you say 'crass' or 'class'?" Bo and Howard heard him whisper and grinned at each other.

The snow splatted against the windshield and the wipers pushed it aside and Mozart poured out of the radio, much to the discomfort of the backseat occupants. Bo looked at Howard's profile as he was concentrating on the road and felt a pure shine inside. She let it be for a moment, then turned it off carefully. From behind her Marvin said, "You guys, uh, want to stop off, don't you?"

Howard sent a questioning glance to Bo. "Anything," she mouthed back.

"Fine," he called to Marvin over the Mozart. "Mitch's Place okay?" There was a muffled giggle from the back and a little Marvin snort.

"I was thinking of David's place." Bo's heart raced, and she checked Howard out of the corner of her eye. If he said no she'd be humiliated, but if he said yes what would they do?

"Kind of cold, isn't it?" Howard said.

"We've all got heaters," Marvin said, and Annette giggled again.

Without another word Howard turned down Lassiter Avenue toward Ellendale Park. Bo caught her breath. In the first place, dumbo, if he were going to make advances he would have by now, and there has never been the slightest indication you are anything more than a good friend who is as fat as he is. Yeah, but . . . he was the one who wanted to double with them. But even if he were going to, he wouldn't do it the first time in front of them. He is too decent, too nice. Only maybe he'll think it's expected and maybe he will because maybe I'm all he can get. Now. She could imagine her mother, red-faced and beside herself with embarrassment. *"Bo, darling, I know today's world is different . . . not that I necessarily approve . . . but I do want to be sure you know . . . I mean you do have to take care . . ."* "Don't worry,

Ma," she could say, *with full reassurance, knowing it was true, "it's not like that at all,"* even though she wished it could be like that, just a little bit. Not to the point of having to take precautions, but . . . good grief, bimbo, where is your fat head taking you? Your object in life is to get him thin and send him back to Cynthia, right? Weezie's face loomed on the windshield and said, *Wrong.* The car stopped suddenly. Bo hadn't even noticed the final loop around the statue of David, the city's pride and the best parking place in town.

"Not many customers tonight," Marvin remarked from the rear.

Bo shivered. "Everybody's home in bed," she said, and immediately could have kicked herself.

"I'm for that," Marvin said. "Trouble is, Annette's mother's against it."

"Marvin, would you cut it out?" Annette said sharply. "Some day somebody's going to take you seriously."

Funny thing. She wants the world to think she's sexy, but God forbid anybody should think she actually Does It, Bo thought to herself and wondered if Annette really Did.

Howard turned off the motor but left the radio on. Bo was grateful because she was at a loss for conversation. Finally she said, "My sister told me that her teacher told her that Armond Levelier's real name is Artie Levitt."

"Armond? . . ." Howard said.

"The premier danseur."

"Oh, right. Artie Levitt, huh? Well it just goes to show you."

"Show you what?" She felt confused.

"I don't know. Something. What's in a name, maybe."

"He also has three children and a wife in Pittsburgh. Which shoots somebody's theory full of holes." She jerked her head backward, but kept her eyes resolutely to the front. She also realized at that moment that they'd both been whispering. Complete silence rose out of the back, then some small sliding sounds, and Bo suddenly understood why Howard had been asked to drive. She bit her thumb and felt terribly hungry. All she could think of to say was, "I'm starved."

"Yeah," Howard said.

Mozart continued to fill the lapses in conversation. At one point Howard turned the volume up and gave her a look of grim amusement. No complaint was heard from behind them. Bo exhausted the topic of the ballet and the things Ms. Albersham had said in class on Thursday. Howard was quieter than usual, and though she wasn't sure, he seemed to be looking at her oddly. More rustling sounds were heard in the rear, and Howard shifted his weight, moving a little closer to her, in a way that could not by any stretch of imagination be called an advance. She looked at him and realized with a shock that he was acutely embarrassed. She understood finally that he'd had to stop when Marvin asked. It would have been a threat to his manhood otherwise. If he did anything now it would mean nothing, nothing at all. Which of course he won't, so why am I worried. But what a spot he's in. How do I get us out? She considered the options, then leaned toward him and whispered, "Do you want to take a walk?"

He looked at her oddly and said quickly, "Why not?"

They opened their doors simultaneously. Annette's voice came through the dark with an edge of franticness. "Where're you going?"

"For a walk," they said together.

"Take your time," Marvin said at the same time as Annette said, "Hurry back."

"Nev, wait a sec," Marvin called just as Howard was closing the door. "You mind changing the station?" Howard reached over and found something sleazier-sounding on the dial and shut the door.

• • •

"Poor Dave," Howard said as they walked around the statue. "Has to be chilly." The statue was wet from snow and there was a light dusting of flakes on David's head, shoulders, and upturned wrist. His marble muscles were outlined in light but his face was hidden in shadows. They stared at his perfection a moment and walked away.

"You know what happened when they got him?" Howard asked as they walked.

"Who?"

"David. The statue. Michelangelo, you know?"

"Oh, yes," Bo said, as if she'd forgotten all about the look of it in the light. "No, what?"

"There was this big fight among the city fathers because he came without a fig leaf. Finally the prudes won, so they added the fig leaf later. Michelangelo was against fig leaves."

"Well, so am I," Bo said, feeling daring. "I mean, the human body is beautiful. What's to hide?" In our case, plenty, she thought.

Howard shook his head. "Crazy story. I think of it every time I drive up . . . every time I go past here," he corrected himself.

How long ago . . . how often . . . with Cyndy, Bo thought. When you looked like that, she thought before she could stop herself, remembering him in his basketball trunks and T-shirt.

"Now," Howard was saying, "the only place you can see him without a fig leaf is to go to Florence and look at the original. I didn't bring it up before, of course, for obvious reasons."

"Yeah, I can hear Marvin now," Bo said, " 'Florence who?' " They both laughed and it sounded loud in the snow. "Oh, wow," Bo said, stopping. An area that was all park grass in the summer stretched out white in front of them, untouched, untrampled, as if nobody'd ever been there before.

"You know what I'm dying to do?" she said after a moment. "Make an angel."

He smiled a go-ahead and she tiptoed, leaving the smallest footprints possible, some distance out into the snow, turned gingerly, and lay down, stretching both arms out to each side. Looking straight above her she could see nothing but a sky full of snow falling directly into her face. She stuck out her tongue like Reenie, to catch some. Raising her head she saw Howard at the edge of the field, still smiling at her. She closed her eyes, lay her head back, and moved her arms and legs in arcs. Her coat made squeaking sounds in the snow.

A minute later came a new set of squeaks to the right of her. She looked over to see Howard flat on his back, doing the same thing. His hand hit hers lightly as the arcs passed each other. "You nut," she sang over the snow to him.

"How do we get up?" he called back.

"Very, very carefully," she said, and did so, slowly. He pulled himself up halfway and sat a minute, breathing hard and wiping the snow from his face. "You have to take the same footprints back," she said. "That's important." She stepped into the half-indentations, holding her arms out for balance. Howard rose from the snow and followed his own prints back to the edge.

"Want to go back?" he asked, nodding in the direction of the car.

"Not really," she said. "What is there about snow that's so cold it makes you warm?"

"You want a scientific answer?"

"Absolutely not," she said, laughing, and began to tramp away from him, kicking snow around left and right. "I love it!" she called. "It's new and it's mine, practically!" She started to prance and bounce, aware that she looked ridiculous and not caring. The sense of the evening was all over her—Reenie in her costume and false eyelashes, blushing when Howard asked her for her autograph—Howard fielding Marvin's awful remarks—her own élan at getting them out of the car when who knows what was going on in the backseat. She felt wildly successful and scared about it. She looked back at Howard who was standing where she'd started from, an edge of black bare trees behind him pointing into the white sky. She held her arms out like a dancer and did a pirouette, the snow all around her, thinking the Snow Queen's music in her head. She did a bunch of ballet movements and then saw Howard moving toward her in an imitation of dancing, bounding and leaping as best he could, looking huge and foolish and wonderful.

"Call me Armond!" he said as he reached her and held out his arm. She took it in both hands and did her idea of an arabesque. They wobbled and slid.

She wound up on her back in the snow with Howard practically on top of her, both of them laughing and unable to stop. "Hey, that's tough!" she said, trying to get up and sliding again.

"You have to take lessons," he said gently. "You're supposed to practice." He was closer to her that minute than he ever had been. The snow was melting in tracks down his face and he had stopped laughing. There was a blank minute full of snow and breathing.

He won't, she thought. He won't, he won't, because it's not like that. Okay, I wish it were, but it's not, and he won't.

He didn't. "We'd better get back," he said in a voice that didn't sound like his. He took her hand to help her up but she knew it didn't mean a thing. They walked back toward the parking area through the snow which was now full of footprints.

"I guess I'd better let my sister do the dancing," Bo said lightly.

"Oh, I don't know," Howard said and smiled at her, but she wasn't looking at him. When they got to the edge of the field she turned and saw the imprints of two fat angels, already filling up with snow.

The car had a thin cover of new white when they got there. "What do we do, knock?" Bo said, her embarrassment coming back. Howard stopped to consider the problem.

"Let's wipe at the windshield a little," he suggested. "That'll give them fair warning." After a decent interval he opened the door on her side, looked in, and nodded to her that it was okay.

She got in, looking casually to the back, and said, "Hi. It's snowing out there."

"No kidding," Marvin said glumly. He and Annette were sitting up straight, not even close to each other. Bo wondered vaguely what had happened but didn't really care. Her stomach felt vacant and the cold had gotten to her. Her boots had leaked and her feet felt wet inside them.

Howard finished wiping the new snow off the car, got in, and started the motor. He also changed the radio back to where it had been before. "FM," Marvin said and made a rude noise. "Fruity music." Nobody said anything. "You guys want to stop at Mitch's now?" Marvin asked as they backed out.

Howard looked to Bo who replied without looking back, "No, I don't think so. I'm not really hungry anymore."

It was an out-and-out lie. As soon as she'd closed the front door to Howard, Bo made for the kitchen and built herself a sandwich with three slices of bread.

Home in his own kitchen Howard surveyed the inside of the refrigerator and found it wanting. Finally he opened the freezer and took out a box of frozen meat patties. He had to take a knife to the side of a bunch of them and was trying manfully to separate them when his father arrived home from a night of poker with colleagues in his department.

"Want one?" Howard said in greeting, twisting the knife and finally popping a patty off the top.

"No thanks," his father said. "Had lots of cheese."

"Cheese," Howard said. "Good idea. Cheeseburger." He moved back to the refrigerator. "—Good night?"

"Six bucks down the drain," his father said, taking off his overcoat and draping it over a kitchen chair to dry.

"You must've been playing for real high stakes, huh?" Howard was carefully peeling the thin white paper off the meat patty.

"How about you?" George Nevelson tried to read his son's face but had never been very good at it. "High stakes?" Howard frowned. "That was simply an oblique way of asking if you had a good time," his father said.

"Sure. We went to the ballet."

"The ballet," his father repeated, and tensed a little, so that Howard knew there was a small pain moving through him.

"I don't care, I think it's lovely. So lovely . . . just the sight of them all in white like that. Before they even move I want to cry. One thing I hope women's lib doesn't ruin is the ballet . . ."

"Good performance?" his father asked, going for the teakettle.

"I guess so. I don't know much about it. They brought the lead dancers in from Pittsburgh."

"Did Barbara like it?"

"Yeah, she liked it a lot," Howard said and turned the front burner on high. It glowed in a blue circle. He brought an iron frying pan down on it. After a minute he dropped the frozen patty into the hot pan. It sizzled and hissed and sent up smoke.

19

The booster club was a curious organization—an In activity in support of supposedly Out values. The *Parkview High School Official Handbook* said it was "devoted to promoting sportsmanship and school spirit." If Dr. Jackson mentioned that sort of thing in a school assembly there was inevitably a mass low-level snicker. But Bo noted that many of the people who sneered were the same ones who showed up every Thursday night in the cafeteria and made pom-poms and posters in support of whatever home team was in season. The right people belonged, and so did everyone else who was looking to rub shoulders with them. It was the biggest club in the school.

Bo had passed these sociological theories on to Howard as they walked there the Thursday after the *Nutcracker* performance. He'd laughed and said, "You've got it wrong, woman. It's not about sportsmanship or any of that stuff. It's about winning."

"Winning what, is the question," Bo said. Howard had

just grinned, reading her as always. She wondered why he still went to the meetings, but didn't ask. She went herself because something told her he wasn't quite safe there alone. She insisted they not sit together, though, so that no one would get the wrong idea. If Howard felt anything about this, he didn't say so.

"Hi. Is that seat taken?" The voice was familiar, but when Bo looked up she drew a blank. The girl smiled as if they'd known each other for years. "I've been wanting to talk to you," she said, and pulled out the chair.

"Me?" Bo said and looked at her curiously.

She was very short, on the pretty side, and carefully put together—hair correctly blow-dried, a yellow Shetland sweater over designer jeans. She wore expensive boots, to which she drew Bo's attention when she sat down, by unzipping them and massaging her ankles. "These are so stiff," she said. "I should've worn one of my other pairs."

Bo had returned her attention to the green and gold crepe paper she was handling, and now, hearing the voice without the face, recognized her—Allison of the ladies' room last fall. She who commiserated with Cyndy: "So he set you free. It's kind of beautiful in a way." Bo had seen this girl around before, of course, in the halls, the cafeteria, at Mitch's, at games. But the members of Cyndy's entourage seemed interchangeable, and she'd never connected one in particular with that voice.

"I mean," the voice said, when Bo hadn't responded, "I always wanted to get to know you. Pass the scissors, would you?"

Allison had clearly settled in to make pom-poms there beside her. Bo looked frantically to the front of the room where Howard was engaged in laughing conversation with several boys in letter sweaters. (He never wore his anymore. She'd offered to remove the letter from the old one and resew it to a larger size, but he'd waved it off as unimportant.)

"Why me?" Bo said, and passed the scissors.

"Why not?" Allison flashed her a smile. It was adorable, practiced, and totally insincere.

"I don't know you, do I?" Bo asked politely.

"I'm Allison Brock. I'm a friend of Cyn's. Cyn Randall? And you," she said, pointing at Bo with the scissors, "are Butter Barrett, right?"

Bo nodded. "I guess I don't know that many seniors."

"Really?" Allison said. "I thought you would by now. Considering. We all know you." She gave an odd little laugh.

"Considering what?" Bo said, unable to stop herself. There was an uncomfortable little ripple working its way through her, like an early-warning system.

"Considering you're going with How. Everybody knows How. He's terrific. Always was," she added and sighed slightly, making it sound a little like something written on a tombstone.

Bo was silent a moment and continued winding green crepe paper around a large piece of heavy cardboard. Allison was doing the same, a step or two behind her. "Could you pass the gold, please?" Bo asked calmly. Allison tossed her the fat ring of gold crepe paper. Bo held one end down and started wrapping the gold around the green she'd finished. When the process was under way she said matter-of-factly, "Howard and I aren't going together."

"You're not," Allison said, not like a question. "You wouldn't kid me, would you?" She gave Bo a suggestive little look that turned her stomach.

"Absolutely not," Bo said.

"Ha!" Allison said and hit the table with her hand. Several pom-pom makers looked up. She lowered her voice, but still sounded triumphant. "*I* was right for a change. Wait'll I tell Cyn. 'Look,' I said to her, 'I'm reasonably sure they're friends, period. Not' . . . well, you know''—Bo flinched—" 'Or what-have-you,' " Allison went on. " 'I mean, you don't see them mooning around or holding hands, right?' But Cyn just thought you wanted to maybe keep that part private. I mean, people can be so rotten, the things they say. Why ask for it, you know? She really wants to see Howard happy, and if you're what makes him happy . . .'' Allison gave a cute little shrug.

Bo had a fantasy of taking the crepe paper and wrapping it around Allison, starting at her head, stuffing the green and gold streamers into her mouth and nose and ears, wrapping them slowly and tightly around her entire body until she looked like a mummy with school spirit.

"Cyn is such a fantastic person," Allison went on without mercy. "I mean I can hardly even believe I'm her friend sometimes. And she was really into Howard. I mean, two years of your life? And when he broke it off with her—it was Howard who did the breaking up, you know, not her—she'd never have done it just because of what happened to him. She'd've stuck by him. I believe that, even if she doesn't. I know her. Nobody knows you like your friends, right? You're wrapping that too tight if you don't mind my saying so.'' Bo looked down at the crepe paper and noted that she was indeed pulling it out of shape. "It won't have any oomph if you stretch it.''

"God forbid,'' Bo said darkly, "that I should produce an oomphless pom-pom.''

Allison apparently didn't hear her. "Anyway, I'm kind of glad to hear I was right about you two," she went on, "because if you want my opinion—now she hasn't said this, but this is what *I* think—I don't think Cyn cares a hoot about Larry Kirby. Of course he's wild about her. Everybody is. Who wouldn't be?'' Bo couldn't think of an answer. "How does Howard feel about her now?'' Allison asked bluntly. "Does he say?''

"We don't talk about things like that." Bo told the truth.

"Could I have the green now?" Bo handed it to her. "All I can say is I have this gut feeling that if Howard were to wiggle his little finger at Cyn she'd come running. Even *now*, with things the way they are. Because she's that terrific a human being. And if *that* happened, I bet How might even get back to being How again, if you follow me." Regretfully, Bo did.

"Not that we don't love him the way he is," Allison went on, "because everybody really does. But we can't help wondering if he's happy, you know? I guess I'm just romantic, but I keep hoping, kind of. And if it did happen they got back together, it probably wouldn't change things for you, would it? I mean, once a friend, always a friend. How has this terrific loyalty, I think, just like Cyn. And she doesn't have a jealous bone in her body, believe me. Are you done with the scissors again, please?"

Repressing the urge to plunge them into Allison's Shetland-covered chest, Bo handed her the scissors. She picked up her own finished pom-pom and waved it tentatively. It drooped a little.

"I can't imagine Cyndy considers me any kind of competition," Bo managed to say, eyes on her pom-pom. "Even if How and . . . even if Howard and I were more than friends, which we are not."

"God only knows," Allison said and rolled her eyes. "I'll tell her, that's all. I'll have to be a little careful about it because if she knew I'd actually asked you she'd die. Absolutely die. And you won't say anything to Howard, will you?"

"No," Bo said simply. "I won't."

"Good," Allison said, beaming and shaking the pom-pom she'd just finished.. "Let nature take its course, I always say. What's supposed to happen will happen, don't you think?''

"Will you excuse me," Bo said, with a little urgency. "I have to go to the bathroom."

20

Annette Morisi had a paneled basement. Weezie always said it was her ticket to popularity. "She wouldn't have any friends at all if she didn't give all the parties. She's probably only having this one to show the world how close she is to Howard the Great's good friend."

"Who's she showing? Darlene? Mary Kay?" Bo asked.

Weezie shrugged. "She only asked them out of habit. Or maybe because they're the only other ones who'll come."

She offered these remarks in Ruthanne's kitchen two nights after Christmas, as Bo was packing food to take with them.

"That's not very nice," Reenie said and looked to her mother for approval.

"I'm sure Louise didn't mean to be unkind," Ruthanne said. She was peeling potatoes.

"I didn't mean anything. I'm just stating the facts."

"If you don't like Annette, why do you go to her parties?"

"Reenie . . ." Ruthanne started to stop her.

"I'm just asking."

"I didn't say I didn't like her, did I?" Weezie said.

"Do you?"

"*Reenie* . . ."

"No," Weezie said after she thought about it.

"Did you get any Oreos, Ma?" Bo had all the cupboards open and was standing on a chair, collecting cracker boxes and diet soda.

"Top shelf behind the oatmeal."

"She hides them," Reenie said proudly.

Bo turned fast and almost lost her balance. "Not from me, Irene Samantha. From you."

"She does not."

"Oh, yes, small one. She doesn't want to see you do disgusting things with them."

"I don't."

"You do!"

"Tell her I don't, Ma!"

Ruthanne picked up another potato and asked Weezie how her mother was.

"She's fine," Weezie said. "What kind of things?" She looked to Reenie. Ruthanne sighed. "What kind of disgusting things can you do with Oreo cookies?" Reenie scowled. Weezie looked to Bo. "I'm fascinated." Ruthanne stabbed at a potato.

"She lets them float in her milk until they're all soggy, and her milk has black crumbs in it when she takes them out."

"That's better than taking them apart and scraping the frosting off with a spoon and eating it and putting them back together with peanut butter."

"I don't do that anymore," Bo said, her face in the cupboard.

"Not much you don't!" Reenie's face was getting red.

"Not often, anyway."

"Anyway, she's not hiding them from me or you. She's hiding them from Howie!" Reenie yelled, slid off her seat, and stomped out.

"Bull's-eye," Weezie said softly as Ruthanne dropped the potato in the waiting pan of water and went after Reenie. "Young lady . . ."

"It's all right, Ma," Bo said to the swinging kitchen door. "No, actually, it's not." She snapped a large brown paper bag open with one motion of her wrist. "But why do I let her get to me that way?"

"Do you really want to know?" Weezie asked.

"Not particularly," Bo sighed.

Weezie went ahead anyway, of course. "Because his Wonderfulness is away and you're uptight about it."

"Baloney," Bo said. "No, salami," and headed toward the refrigerator.

She refused to be upset over the fact that Howard and his father had been forced by zealous Aunt Marcia to spend their Christmas in Syosset. It wasn't as if he'd wanted to go. "It's a family time," he'd mimicked to Bo privately, "and for better or worse Donald and Jason and Jeremy and I are your family and I won't enjoy my Christmas if I think you're both bathing in won ton soup or something." It had been easier to go, Bo knew. Easier for them, anyway. She rummaged in the refrigerator, saying back to Weezie, "No, really. I miss him, sure, because I'm used to him, but it's no big deal."

"Right." Weezie said. "And since when do you and baby sister have words?"

"Since she has become an adorable little pain in the tail."

"She always was. When did you notice?"

"I don't know. She's just gotten hostile lately," Bo said, tossing the Oreos into the bag.

"How lately?"

"The last couple of months." Weezie raised an eyebrow but said nothing. Bo tossed more things into the paper bag—her pajamas and the toiletries kit she'd brought from upstairs.

"How come you don't use your new overnight bag?"

"Because it's too new and too good," Bo said crossly.

"And from Howie for Christmas," Weezie finished.

"I just don't want any comments from anybody. It's real leather."

"Which means . . ."

"Nothing." Bo glared at her and threw a mottled notebook into the bag.

"What's that?"

"My journal."

"You're going to write? What are you going to do—observe us all? That quaint tribal custom, the slumber party?"

"I don't know. I just know I carry it with me or else *she'll* get into it. She reads at third-grade level, you know. Even handwriting. Ma taught her. Just what the kid needed, a head start."

"What is it, X-rated?" Weezie nodded toward the top of the notebook which protruded from the bag.

"Louise, don't start. I've told you three zillion times . . ."

". . . It's platonic. I know."

"It is. Howard is a good friend. The best friend I . . ." Bo stopped to retrieve her foot from her mouth.

"It's okay." Weezie waved her on. "You think I begrudge you? Anyway, boy *friends* and girl *friends* are somewhat different." She kept her face a mask, but Bo wasn't looking. "Tell me more about your sister."

"What's to tell? I'm not her favorite person anymore."

"Who is? Howie?"

"On alternate days."

"She's jealous," Weezie offered.

"Could you knock off the dime-store-shrink stuff, dearie?"

Weezie shrugged. "Takes one to know one, I guess."

Bo stopped in her tracks on her way to the refrigerator, turned, and looked at her friend. "Bear with me, would you, Louise? Just till I get him through this? We're going to start a diet right after he gets back from his Aunt's. This is kind of a last fling for me." She nodded toward a small salami that she took from the refrigerator and added to the bag.

Weezie, who was sorry she'd said so much, looked carefully at the National logo on the brown bag. "Maybe Reenie's not hostile," she said. "Maybe you're not reading her right."

"I would say her giving me a Miss Piggy calendar for Christmas was definitely hostile."

"Last year you would have thought it was funny."

"Last year was different," Bo said, and slammed the refrigerator door.

"Hey, that hurts!" Weezie yelled. "Those dumb things are hot."

"That's why they're called hot rollers," Annette said and jabbed a giant pin into Weezie's scalp.

"What are you trying to do to me!"

"You asked me to," Annette said, pushing another pin in with some satisfaction.

"I asked you to set my hair, not to maim me." The roller hung a moment as short strands of hair escaped, then it slipped out again and rolled hotly down Weezie's neck. "Ow!" she yelled again. "What is this? Some new form of medieval torture?"

"It won't work," Annette said, and pulled a few rollers out of the top of Weezie's hair, leaving it in raised lumps. "God, your hair's thin. Besides which, it's not long enough."

"It has to be. I'm letting it grow out." Weezie looked at herself in the mirror and suppressed a groan.

"Have you told it?" Annette asked, sorting the rollers out by size.

"Very funny. You don't talk to hair."

"Why not?" Bo said from a corner. She was munching Oreos, which were raising her spirits. "People talk to plants."

Weezie moved closer to the mirror and ran her fingers through the lumps of hair. Her scalp shone in bright pink patches. She held a lock of hair out to its full two-inch length. (She'd had it cut three times since September, each time more disastrously.) "I've been meaning to mention to you, hair . . . You're not too terrific." She dropped the lock and it fell limply back. "So what's the difference. Looks don't count, right? Beauty is only skin deep! Real beauty comes from within! Excuse me a minute, folks, and I'll glow for you." She wiggled her fingers as if she were connected electrically.

"You sound like my mother," Bo said, trying to laugh. "Did yours tell you that?"

"No," Weezie said. "She bought me a book on it."

"I notice you read it," Annette said.

Mary Kay winced and said, "Weezie, your hair isn't that bad. It'll grow. I bet by the Valentine Ball you'll be able to get it in rollers again. Maybe even get a perm."

"Fresh fuzz," Weezie replied. "Goody." She looked at the mirror again but had stopped clowning.

"I mean it," Mary Kay said, and it was clear she did. "You shouldn't run yourself down all the time."

"You know something, Mary Kay?" Weezie said. "You are very kind. Pathologically kind, in fact."

"Are you saying it's sick to be nice?" Darlene looked shocked.

"Speaking of books . . ." Annette was headed across the room. "I've got this terrific one I've been saving for you all. The ones who need it . . ." she said pointedly toward Weezie. "What a sketch. It was my mother's when she was, like, our age? If you believe that.'' Giggling, she reached behind a shelf of paperbacks and drew out a book with a shocking-pink cover. On it a girl in a blue checked dress was holding a daisy to her cheek. In lacy letters the title read *How to Be a Girl*.

"Why were you hiding it? What is it, pornography?" Weezie said.

"Are you kidding? They didn't even know about sex in the fifties."

"Yeah, I'd heard it was a recent discovery," Bo said.

"Listen," Annette said, waving for quiet. "This is an incredible relic. 'Girls,' " she read, " 'are quite different from boys.' "

"Columbus!" Weezie shouted.

"Hallelujah," Darlene added loudly, surprising them all. She blushed.

"Come on, listen," Annette went on. " 'Whatever role you choose for yourself in life—career woman or, simply and nobly' . . . get that, nobly . . . 'wife and mother, you will want to make the most of yourself as a woman. This book will tell you how.' "

"Thank God!" Bo put out, getting into the spirit of things. "Well, don't stop now."

"It's too much," Annette said. "Isn't it too much? Of course there's a page and a half about looks-don't-really-count and you-should-work-for-that-inner-glow you were mentioning, Louise, but then the whole rest of the book is this long set of directions on how to make the most of yourself, lookswise and personalitywise. I mean there's a whole section in here about how to take a bath, for God's sake. And seven pages on how to have beautiful feet—but, get this, only three pages on your legs. How come, I wonder."

"Maybe her husband had a foot fetish," Weezie offered.

"Whose?" Darlene asked.

"The author's, Dar," Mary Katherine said patiently. "What's her name?"

" 'Betsy Bennett Bradley,' " Annette read from the cover. "She must be dead by now, don't you think?"

"Of a chill," Bo said. "From spending all her time in the bathtub."

"No," Weezie put in. "She got hit by a truck while crossing the street looking at her feet."

"Go on, read some more," Darlene said and nobody contradicted her.

"Well . . ." Annette was leafing through the book. "There's a long number on figure types and how to pick your clothes."

"Oh, goody," Bo said. "What's it say for me? Figure type: Fat."

"It doesn't say fat. It says heavy."

"Naturally. What am I supposed to wear?"

"Lemme see . . ." Annette turned the pages quickly and stopped. " 'Heavy*set*,' it says. She recommends quiet good taste."

"Oh, that's me," Bo said, sweeping an arm over her shirt and jeans.

"Says watch out for shorts and slacks. I think she means don't wear them."

"That'll attract attention."

"She says thin up-and-down stripes will minimize the disaster areas."

"Thank you very much."

". . . No checks or plaids."

"There goes the rest of my wardrobe. Does she specify what quiet good taste means?"

". . . Well, not exactly. Except your bathing suit should have a skirt and you should pick out small accessories."

"Good. I'll borrow my sister's purse."

"What about me?" Weezie asked.

"I thought you didn't care," Annette said.

"I thought this was a joke," Weezie growled.

"Okay," Annette said, not very graciously. "Let's see . . . figure type, short and skinny. I mean, 'petite and slender' . . . very *nice* book . . ." Weezie waited, glaring, as Annette read, muttered, and grinned. "You're not going to believe this. It says . . . Louise, it says you're a cute *widget*. I kid you not, that's what it says. You can be 'birdlike,' ye Gods! and 'entrancing' . . ."

"What bird, does it specify?" Weezie asked. "A penguin, maybe. I'll borrow my dad's tails."

"It doesn't say what bird. A canary, maybe. A vulture?"

"Vultures aren't petite," Darlene said.

"Oh, I guess she means you can wear bright colors, yeah, and wait a minute . . ." Annette read on. "This doesn't make sense. It says *you* can wear up-and-down stripes. Wasn't that for fat?"

"Both," Weezie said, draping an arm around Bo and moving them both to the mirror. "They won't be able to tell us apart." Bo looked at the two of them and for a moment had the sensation they were in a funhouse in front of one of those wavy mirrors that send back trick images. Weezie looked about three feet tall, a foolish-faced dwarf hugging a lady elephant.

"Oh, wait . . ." Annette was still giggling and reading. "This you will love. It says you might mind being short, but think of what an advantage it is—'you make the lads'—lads, yet!—'feel big and powerful.' "

"*That* I hadn't noticed," Weezie said. She left Bo staring at her reflection and turned wide-eyed, clasping her hands dramatically in front of her, "Oh, Thir, Thir, thave me, thave me!—is this for real?" She held out her hand for the book.

"It's in print," Annette said, handing it over. Bo hadn't moved from the mirror. The more she looked the more she seemed expanded and misshapen. She stared at herself a long time.

Weezie flipped through *How to Be a Girl,* shaking her head. "I guess generations of females read this stuff and believed it. When I think of the sick games they had to play!"

"When was liberation?" Darlene asked.

"Somewhere around the sixties, wasn't it?" Mary Kay offered.

"It wasn't." Bo's voice was suddenly loud in the room. She had turned from the mirror and she wasn't smiling. They looked at her as if she'd grown a second head.

"Women's liberation," she went on—it was her tone that unnerved them—"who's kidding who? Whom, I beg your pardon, Darlene. Oh, sure, maybe now you have more women telephone men and girls can get into welding school, but the cosmetic companies are still cleaning up, you notice? Skin deep my foot! Liberation, ladies, is a crock!"

"But, Butter," Darlene started, sure that right was on her side, "what about that essay you read in class? Ms. Albersham loved it. Women are more liberated than men? Men should be able to cry? You said that, didn't you?"

"I was out of my gourd, is all," Bo said. "Why should men cry? What have they got to cry about? They're still calling the shots, aren't they? I mean . . ." She stopped for a minute, caught her breath, and tried to cancel out the picture of Howard she had in her head. Howard with snow on his face, very close to her. "I mean . . ." She stomped over and took the book from Weezie, waving it. ". . . The fifties were at least honest. A little number like this told you what was what. If you brushed your teeth and took enough bubble baths you had the inside track to Popularity Plus. It doesn't matter if you're not gorgeous, but here's what to do. Now then, today we have this so-called liberation, but you've still got your magazines like *Glamour*, right? When I was over at your place yesterday," she directed herself to Weezie, "I noticed your sister had a copy."

"My sister," Weezie defended, "is twenty-two years old and going for a masters in medieval lit. She only had that thing because somebody left it on a bus or something."

"Right," Bo said, as if it proved her point. "But one way or another, Jennifer Schultz, giant female intellect, was in possession of *Glamour* magazine. Liberated version, of course."

"You looked at it, too, didn't you?" Annette said.

"Of course I did!" Bo said, raising her voice slightly. "Believe it or not, friends, I am also a female person. Cover to cover I looked at it. Oh, yes, full of articles on the executive look and how to pick out your first briefcase, but basically"—she waved the book again—"they're still telling us how to look the look, how to catch a man. That hasn't changed in, what, thirty years?" She tossed the book at the couch and sighed. "Two hundred. A millennium."

"Oh, but the attitudes are different," Annette said. "Everything's more modern. They talk about sex and everything right out. I mean, look at *Cosmo*."

"I can't," Darlene said. "My mother won't let me have it in the house."

"*Cosmo*'s got sex on the brain," Weezie said. "So do you, Morisi." Annette was unfazed.

It was Bo who spoke, and her voice was a little threatening. "So do we all, dear heart." She looked straight at Weezie. "Even thou."

"Where did you get that?" Weezie whirled around, incensed.

"Why did you want Annette to do your hair?"

"To be sociable. And because I have crummy hair."

"And why do you care if you've got crummy hair?"

"Not because I'm trying to get laid!" There was a double gasp in the corner from Darlene and Mary Katherine.

133

The phone rang. Everyone was grateful. Weezie, who was closest to it, picked it up. It was a telephone store phone, a version of Snoopy that Annette's mother had thought would be just adorable for a rec room. "Yeah?" Weezie said nastily. "—I mean, Morisi residence. . . . Yeah, she's here." She gave a little smirk and motioned to Bo. "It's for you. Your platonic relationship, calling from Long Island."

Howard had called to ask her to a New Year's Eve party.

"I thought he wasn't going to be here," Annette said when Bo told them. She had remarked to Bo earlier that they were both holiday widows. "I thought you said he had to be with his relatives."

"I did," Bo said. "I mean he did. You know how that kind of thing is."

"Really," Annette sighed. "Marvin didn't want to go with his folks either, but what could he do?"

"Yeah," Weezie said. "I heard they dragged him kicking and screaming all the way to St. Thomas."

Annette ignored her and stayed fixed on Bo. "But didn't you say How wouldn't be back till the third?"

"Well, he wasn't supposed to be," Bo said, trying to look like the whole thing didn't matter, "but he got this call down *there* asking him to a party up *here*, and his aunt thought that was so terrifically healthy she let him off the hook. He's flying in on the cheapo airline Thursday morning."

"What about his dad?"

"He's got to stay. Aunt Marshmallow insists he shouldn't be alone on New Year's Eve."

"She sounds like a busybody," Weezie said. "Doesn't Mr. Nevelson have anything to say about it?"

"I guess he said okay."

"I can never understand it," Darlene said, "when people who are adults do things they don't really want to do."

134

"Neither can I," Bo said. "But my mother says I will when I get there."

"So, where's the party?" Annette said impatiently.

Bo turned color. That was the question she had hoped to avoid, though she knew she couldn't. Why had her mother told him to call her here, in front of everybody?

"I thought I knew all the parties that were going on," Annette said, frowning. "Tippy Carmichael's having one—which I wouldn't be caught dead at. She's inviting absolutely anybody. And of course the Y is doing their dumb thing—sherbet in ginger-ale punch and Cheez Whiz all over everything." She shuddered and then looked embarrassed, realizing that that was where Darlene and Mary Katherine could probably end up. "—And Julie Newman's having a do—that's where Marvin and I would've been if he were in town."

"Oh, sure," Weezie said.

"As it stands, I'd rather make a bundle baby-sitting," Annette went on, ignoring her again. "The only other party I know is . . . Well, it couldn't be *that* one." She dismissed the possibility with a wave. There was a quiet moment.

"No!" Annette said and looked stunned.

"You got it," Bo said and reached for the Oreos.

"No!" Annette said again. "It's too bizarre! Why?!"

"Something about old-time's sake."

"What's he up to?" Weezie said, catching on.

"What's *she* up to?" Annette said. Darlene and Mary Katherine looked confused, then figured it out.

Bo said nothing. She was carefully disjoining her Oreo cookie. She scraped the white icing off with her tongue and set the bare halves on her knee. "Annette, do you have any peanut butter?" she asked, as if it were the only thing on her mind.

21

*T*he party was at Cynthia Randall's house. They rode toward it without saying much. George Nevelson's aged Impala (Marion had been driving the Dart last May) did not have FM on its radio. "Get something, would you?" Howard said, flicking the control on. Static crackled into the silence. Bo was reminded of mornings last fall, waiting for his voice to come over the P.A. She turned the dial quickly, sliding it over several stations until she found a tolerable one. Slick strings and a harp slid all over a song she recognized as one her mother sang to the dishes now and then, something about remembering April and being glad.

Bo felt awful. She didn't know why, but she had a strong sense that whatever it was she and Howard had—the friendly need, the sense of collaboration, of protection, the unexplained laughter between them—was going to end tonight. She thought of "Mmm-smooth" and snow angels and Halloween with Reenie tripping around in a tattletale gray sheet while she and Howard checked over her trick-or-treat loot for apples with hidden razor blades. (There hadn't been any, and when the bag had passed inspection Reenie had offered it to them generously. They'd taken miniature Mars bars.)

How can I give him back before I've fixed him? Bo thought, the sadness spreading all over her. Weight Watchers, she'd figured, or maybe Overeaters Anonymous. They'd do it together, as soon as he was ready. Howard stopped the car. They had to park halfway down the block. "Big party," he remarked as he slammed the door and looked at the line of cars parked ahead of them.

The Randall home was a large half-stone house in the best part of town. There were footprints all over the snow that covered the lawn. "We might as well go in the side," Howard said. "I'm sure the shindig's downstairs. Mrs. Randall has a thing about her wall-to-wall." They walked halfway around the house, which had a side lawn, too, a double lot. Howard's familiarity with the layout made her miserable. He was whistling, with a wide vibrato, the melody from the car as he rang the bell.

Cyndy was an artist and had made clever little signs for all over the party. One directed where to put coats and another pointed the way to the Comfort Station. This was illustrated by an old-fashioned outhouse with a moon on the door, drawn in magic markers. It took a while for Bo to see the signs because the room was very dark, illuminated entirely by a series of candles. "She collects them," Howard explained, making Bo feel worse. There were thin ones, fat ones, decorative ones—a trio of angels, a mushroom, an ice-cream cone, even a fake Twinkie with a wick in it—as well as a lot of little candles set in jelly jars. They all seemed to be scented, and the room smelled variously of bayberry, cinnamon, lemon, lily of the valley, and other candle perfumes, mixed with the strong smell of salami and provolone cheese.

There were three punch bowls lined up, each with its own clever label. A purple fizzy liquid with pineapple chunks in it and foam indicating melted sherbet was labeled Nursery School and illustrated with a smiling Little Bo-Peep. The middle bowl held a winy-looking liquid with orange slices floating in it and maraschino cherries frozen into ice cubes. The label read Golden Glow and featured a blushing smiling sun. The third bowl contained an amber liquid with no ice. Its label bore a skull and crossbones and was marked Killer Diller. Bo looked at it and wondered where Cyndy's parents were.

"There's food," Cyndy had said as she ushered them in, as if they might be worried about it. She'd given Howard a warm hug of greeting and acted as if Bo were some sort of celebrity. "I've heard sooo much about you . . ." Bo wondered when they'd talked. "That dress is fantastic!" Cyndy added, smiling adorably. What does she mean, Bo thought. Fantastically large? Fantastically Out? Cyndy looked sensational in blue stirrup pants and an oversized sweatshirt that looked to have been spray-painted with some sort of silvery stuff, a small silver Christmas ornament in her hair.

Bo's Indian-style caftan had been bought that afternoon in a last desperate run to the mall with her mother. Lane Bryant had had nothing left but chiffon tents. Then Ruthanne had had an idea and, sure enough, they'd found something—in the cruisewear section of the maternity boutique. The fact that the dress had vertical stripes was entirely a coincidence.

The featured food was a six-foot submarine sandwich, which took up the whole length of the table. It had been sliced into manageable portions, and without asking them, Cyndy put two slices on paper plates and handed them over, along with napkins which read, "Another year? What's the Big Deal?"

"Don't be shy," Cyndy said, nodding to the giant sub. "There's another six feet in the kitchen. Now drinks. I know what *you* want," she said to Howard. "Barbara, listen, don't be embarrassed and feel like you have to be sociable. Not everybody here is a senior." She said it so sweetly and with such sincerity that it took Bo a minute to be irritated, and by that time Cyndy had returned with a glass of Nursery School for her and Killer Diller for Howard. Bo raised an eyebrow at him, but he wasn't looking at her.

"Howie, you'll introduce Bo around, won't you? He knows everybody." Cyndy winked disarmingly at them both as if they all knew something funny, gave an enchanting little laugh, and went to answer the door again. How does she do it? Bo wondered to herself. How can she be so cool and warm and beautiful and friendly and totally easy with them? Because, bimbo, she thought, she doesn't take you seriously. You're some kind of aberration—like Howie's fat—that she's counting on to be temporary.

How did she have the nerve to ask him, though, when everybody knows they were a pair last year? Was it a game? A mean joke? A sort of display of what had happened to him and look-what-he's-got-*now*, meaning Bo? She doubted it. Cyndy seemed too genuinely nice for that. (*"Does a nice girl serve Killer Diller punch at her parties? I'm just asking,"* Bo heard her mother say in her head.)

Bo bit hard on the sub to keep away her worst thoughts, but it didn't work. Was it a signal? All is forgiven, Howie, come home, fat or not? And even if she didn't mean that, suppose he thought she did? What about Larry Kirby? He certainly didn't look threatened. He was walking around with a big bowl of Fritos looking very much a part of the management. Was it her imagination, or did he offer them to Howard more often than to anybody else?

Bo finished her punch and made a face before she could stop herself. It was mostly grape soda.

"Want some more?" Howard asked. It was the first thing he'd said to her in a while. He'd been standing there eating and drinking and blandly surveying the action, looking as if he were perfectly comfortable. "How about some of the real thing?" he offered.

"The middle one, maybe," she said. "Do I dare?"

"I'll tell them you're precocious," Howard said. He grinned at her and for a minute she thought the evening might not be a disaster after all. He came back with a glass of Golden Glow and another of Killer Diller for himself.

"Howeee!" a high-pitched cracked voice came from behind them. "Do I finally get to meet the girlfriend?" Well, Bo thought, feeling the heat rise to her face, he can't very well correct somebody on the spot right in front of me. They turned and there was Dodson L. White.

Up close he seemed taller and skinnier, his cheeks impossibly pink, his very yellow hair cut short. "Hello-ho-ho," he said. The standard greeting, now fondly imitated all over Parkview. Doddie, somehow, by virtue of being sure of who he was and not caring much what anybody made of it, had made the transition from an In misfit to an In person, accepted totally, mannerisms, eccentricities and all. It mystified Bo, but somewhere she could understand it. After all, Howard seemed to be making the reverse trip.

Doddie White extended his hand to Bo and beamed. His cheeks looked even pinker. "I know who *you* are, but we have never been properly introduced. I'm Doddie White."

"I know," was all Bo could think of to say. He pumped her right hand so hard that the punch she was holding in her left sloshed out. "He's been hiding you from us," Doddie said, making scolding sounds at Howard.

"Oh, I don't think so," Bo said, extricating her hand. "That would be pretty tough."

Doddie threw back his head and laughed the loud cackling sound that reminded Bo of the Wicked Witch of the West. "I love it! She's big and beautiful and funny, too!" He said it without a drop of ill will. "Nevelson, you're a lucky fellow." He gave Howard a poke where his ribs would be and moved on, still beaming. "Toodle-oo," he said over his shoulder.

"He's an original," she started to say, but Howard had disappeared. She looked over and saw him back at the punch bowl.

Okay, she thought, fine. Maybe if I just circulate alone people won't take us for granted so much. And if he wants to send *her* a signal, I won't have to watch . . .

She took a deep breath and moved into the mainstream of the party as if she were swimming. The faces were familiar, mostly the Parkview famous, in fact, but there was no one she knew well enough to just talk to. The music was enormous and the wall paneling seemed to be thumping with the bass. At one end of the room some people were dancing. Bo couldn't dance in the modern way; at least she'd never allowed herself to make the public spectacle of trying. When she was small her mother had taught her the standard ballroom steps of her own youth and Bo did them well, but nobody had ever invited her onto the floor. She supposed Howard would have to before the evening was out and she was glad that the room was as dark as it was. As for the no-hands-and-jiggle-around school of dancing, which was what her father called it, she had tried it in the privacy of her living room, and had laughed herself sad and silly at the sight mirrored in the glass bookcase.

She floated by small knots of people, all of whom seemed so involved that it would be impossible to dive into their ongoing conversations. That they were managing to talk at all above the music amazed her. She watched Cyndy move from group to group, effortlessly joining and leaving them, giving people a squeeze or a pat or a knowing, charming little giggle.

Bo moved, too, occasionally glancing over her shoulder, congratulating herself for her independence. She would find a chair or a pillar and stand behind it or lean against it for a while, a look on her face that she hoped was fascinated. She picked up odd objects and examined them raptly—an ashtray made of a miniature rubber tire, Goodyear stamped on it; a wooden box with small shells arranged on the top spelling out San Juan; a candle shaped like a fried egg. She would study each thing intelligently as if it held some grave inner meaning, then would set it down with a thoughtful frown and proceed to the next hiding place, always hoping somebody might stop her and say hello.

There was an appealing corner behind the dance floor and she moved toward it nonchalantly, but she was stopped by a familiar voice coming from a Barcolounger, facing, thankfully, the other way. ". . . Cyn gives the most *incredible* parties, don't you think? I mean the *atmosphere* . . ." Bo made a quick turn out of the line of vision of Allison Brock.

She had progressed nearly all the way around the room now. Nobody seemed to notice, least of all Howard. Well, why should he? He'd only brought her here because he had to.

She helped herself to a black olive from a dish nearby and looked around for somewhere to put the pit. As if by magic an ashtray appeared in front of her nose. It was held by a hand that was attached to, of all people, David Abraham. His hair was wilder than ever and he wore a brown cardigan sweater with pockets and several moth holes in the front of it. "Thanks," she said and dropped the pit in. The ashtray disappeared. "I didn't know you knew Cynthia."

"I don't," he said. "Not really. I read a paper on Nietzsche to the humanities club just before Christmas. She's the treasurer. Organization type. I ran into her in the drug-store Christmas Eve—that's when I do what shopping I'm forced to—and she goes and invites me to this party she's having. I think I'm supposed to be the token intellectual.'' As if to prove the point he took a pipe out of his pocket, filled it, and tried several times to light it, but it kept going out. "How about you?" he said, puffing strenuously.

"I'm here with a friend," Bo said, and nodded across the room to where Howard was wedged between the wall and the punch table.

"Oh, yeah," David said, acknowledging she wasn't sure what.

"Are you enjoying yourself?" Bo asked, for lack of anything else to say.

David shrugged. "Whatever that means."

Bo looked around at the faces, the flickering lights over them, and the changing shadows on the wall, which kept time to the relentless music. It occurred to her that she'd always meant to read Dante's "Inferno." "Why'd you come, then?" she said, really wondering. "I'm just asking."

"Interesting question," David said, puffing. The pipe had finally gotten going. He took it out of his mouth and looked at it a minute. "I didn't have anything else to do. And I figured it might make good material." He patted his pocket, from which protruded the top of a small spiral notebook and a Bic. Bo smiled. "What's funny?" David asked soberly.

"I don't know," she said. "I've got one, too, in my pocket." She pointed to the side of the caftan, below her waist. "Just the idea of a lot of people going ahead and living while some of us stand around and make notes about it . . ." David didn't smile.

Someone had changed the record and slowed things down. Bo recognized the mellow antique sound of the Four Freshmen, singing in the sort of harmony that made her think life must have been simpler back then.

"I beg your pardon . . ." A voice moved in. Like the ashtray, Doddie White had materialized in front of her just when she needed him. "Would the lady care to dance?" Bo nodded an excuse-me to David and followed Doddie out to the dance floor, an area of linoleum roughly five feet square. He held out his arms, like an Arthur Murray poster, and she walked into them.

"You dance divinely," he said in his squeaky voice. She looked up and saw he wasn't trying to be funny.

"Thank you," she murmured. "My mother taught me. I haven't had much practice, though."

"Naughty Howard. I'll tell him he should take you dancing once a week." Oh, listen, she wanted to say, about me and Howie . . . We're not . . . But then she decided to skip it.

He was easy to follow, with a grace that was unexpected in such a long skinny body. We must be quite a sight together, she thought, but maybe because of the punch didn't much care. Only one other couple was dancing, and they weren't holding each other the classical way, but had their arms sort of wrapped around each other's hips. They didn't seem to be dancing so much as rocking slowly from side to side, making barely perceptible movements across the floor. Doddie looked at them, then winked broadly at her. He executed a few surprise steps which she followed easily. The music was over disappointingly soon. She'd been hoping he would end with an old-fashioned dip, but he didn't. Probably afraid he'd drop me, she figured.

"Thank you," he said with a little bow. "I hope you'll save me another." She smiled and said she'd be delighted. I don't know what else I'd do with it, she thought, and looked casually around the room for Howard, hoping he might have noticed them. She couldn't see him. Well, she'd held her own without him for a change, and that felt like something—

she wasn't sure what. She surveyed the room again. He didn't seem to be anywhere. Then, hating herself for it, she looked around for Cynthia but couldn't find her, either. She headed for the punch table and poured herself another Golden Glow.

The punch and food were in an alcove and the hallway to the bathroom was just beyond it. The walls were nothing but plasterboard, so Bo heard the following exchange easily:

"Hello-ho-ho. Lovely party."

"Oh, Doddie, honestly, you're a prince." It was Cynthia's voice. "I wouldn't have asked you, but you know you're a trendsetter. Now everybody will dance with her and it'll be just fine."

Bo set down her punch cup steadily, untouched. There was the sound of a little kiss, a smack on the cheek. "My pleasure," Doddie squeaked. Bo could see the little bow he must be making. "She's a nice girl—no, really, she is."

"Well, you're about the nicest person alive."

Doddie must have continued on to the bathroom. Cynthia emerged from the hall and walked straight into the inferno, looking very pleased with herself. She was carrying a plastic clothes basket full of hats and noisemakers. "Ten to twelve!" she shouted. "Larry, turn on the TV." It was an old set and the color was terrible. The Times Square crowd emerged slowly in mostly pink, with green faces. An announcer said, "It's seven minutes to the New Year, folks." "My watch must be off," Cyndy said above the din. "Let's synchronize." Those who cared to adjusted their watches, and Cyndy, with Larry's help, passed out the New Year's equipment.

"Hat?" Larry said to Bo as he passed her. She hadn't moved but was standing there the way Howard had been before, wedged between the table and the wall. Where was he now? "Hat?" Larry said again and held out a selection.

145

She picked out a blue one (to set off my eyes, she thought grimly) and stared at it a minute—blue foil, glitter all over it—then calmly pulled the elastic under her chin. "Where's Howard?" Larry asked as he pulled out a horn for her.

"Upstairs," she said, although she hadn't the slightest idea. She didn't, in fact, care if she ever saw Howard Nevelson again in her lifetime. He'd taken her there because he had to, and she knew perfectly well he had disappeared to avoid the mandatory midnight kiss. Well, she wasn't going to stand here in a dumb hat blowing a dumb horn and being humiliated any further. She thought of hiding under the punch table, which had a long paper tablecloth over it, but she was afraid somebody would see her crawling under there.

"Two minutes to twelve!"—the TV announcer was getting excited—"and as always there's a lot of happy people here in Times Square, New York City. We take you now to the Grand Ballroom of the . . ." Bo decided the bathroom was her best bet and moved quickly down the hall. Someone was in there and the door was locked. She went back into the party room quickly—everybody's eyes were on the TV set so nobody noticed—and moved up the stairs into the main part of the house. She passed the darkened parlor and went up another set of stairs. Mrs. Randall's burnt orange wall-to-wall cushioned her steps all the way.

"TEN . . . NINE . . . EIGHT . . . SEVEN . . . SIX . . ." The voice of the Times Square crowd augmented by the members of Cyndy Randall's party reached all the way to the second floor. A door was open a few inches and a light was on and Bo could see a tile wall and the edge of a towel. With relief she pushed at the door, but something was in the way. She pushed again and heard a moan. She opened the door sufficiently to put her head through and saw Howard passed out on the bathroom floor.

"THREE . . . TWO . . . ONE . . . HAPPY NEW YEAR!" everybody raved and started singing. " 'SHOULD

146

AULD ACQUAINTANCE BE FORGOT AND NEVER BROUGHT TO MIND . . .' ''

Working from below she was able to bend his legs to allow her entry. He was stretched out with his head near the bottom of the toilet. He had thrown up on Mrs. Randall's blue plush bath mat and all over himself.

Instinctively she started to clean up. She pulled a long wad of toilet paper out and lifted his head and tried to wipe off his face. His eyes opened. "Happy New Year, Howard," she said.

He stared at her blankly, moaned, and closed his eyes again.

'' 'WE'LL TAKE A CUP OF KINDNESS YET FOR AULD LANG SYNE . . .' ''

Bo looked at Howard a moment, ran a finger over his forehead, and let his head drop gently back on the mat. Then she made a decision. She got up, leaving the rest of the mess, and went downstairs to dance.

There was confetti, streamers and small bits of it, all over the room. The TV was still on, and the couples on the floor were moving to the sounds of the grand ballroom band. Cyndy was right. As soon as Bo entered, someone asked her to dance. She only knew him by sight—a dark-haired boy named Steven Untermeier, who went out for track. "Aha, a trend-follower," she said. He looked puzzled but led her onto the dance floor.

He was followed by Corey Becker, Chris Dougherty, and Arthur Ingraham. Several of them seemed a little drunk, but Bo didn't mind. She was intent on having a very good time. She smiled a lot and emitted quite a golden glow, despite the fact that she was avoiding the punch, since she'd probably have to get herself home. Nobody seemed to miss Howard at all, but every time Bo thought of him lying up there, rage and humiliation ran through her like Killer Diller.

Somebody switched the TV set off and put on a loud fast record. Arthur Ingraham apologized and said he couldn't do that kind of thing. Bo waved him away but the beat made her twitch. She wanted to dance fast, no hands, and looked around for a partner. Everybody seemed matched. She saw David Abraham lolling in a beanbag chair, just watching. She danced over to him, all the way across the floor (couples parted like the Red Sea), and held out her hands to him. "No way," he said.

"Come on, Hemingway, just for the experience." He put down his pipe and let her pull him up. The music thumped diligently and Bo did her idea of what went with it. David was stiff, kept his arms straight down, but his feet moved well, like a boxer's. "See," Bo called over the sound, "you're better than you thought! So am I! It's easy!"

The candles still burned at various heights in the room, casting the same weird shadows. Bo was amazed at how good it felt to move. Her body didn't seem heavy; it seemed cooperative, the excess flesh moving whichever way she did, following her in little ripples. The music and the low light and the sense of Hell and of Howard upstairs took over. She moved everything—her knees, her belly, her bust, her elbows, her hands, her head. She felt at once connected with everybody, only higher, larger than anyone there.

She was dimly aware that David had given up and left the floor and that she might be making the feared spectacle of herself, but even the spectacle felt wonderful. Words flew into her head like bats: With Howard out cold I am the most powerful person here. She moved all around in a circle, shaking her head wildly. "She's drunk," she heard somebody say. "No, I'm not," she called back. The floor started to clear and people were clapping. She clapped herself and moved backward, flinging her head from side to side, her hair rising like spun gold over her shoulders. She bumped backward into a piece of furniture but didn't stop for a second. There was a scream. ''My God, she's on fire!''

The smell of burning hair rose in the room. There were flames in the corner of her eye and heat all around her. The next thing she knew she was on her knees and Cyndy Randall was beating the back of her head with a pillow.

22

"So," Victor said, removing the shocking-pink drape from around her as if this were an unveiling, "I always said you had too much a mop. Now we see a pretty face."

"There are those," Bo said, staring at her short-haired self in the mirror, "who say I have too much a face."

"Look the back." Victor spun her around and gave her a hand mirror. She eyed the back of her neck. There was a red patch on it that extended down into her collar. Her hair was gold against it, wavier now that it was short and shaped close to her head. She felt exposed and light-headed.

"Now you will have to wash the neck," Victor said with a broad wink. She tried to smile, knowing he expected it. "I'm laughing," he said, meaning, I'm joking. "A pretty neck. Good skin. I have customers—for a skin like that—" He made a throat-slitting motion. Bo blinked.

• • •

"I would absolutely die for a skin like yours," Cyndy said as she applied an ice pack to Bo's neck. They were up in Cyndy's bedroom. The sounds of the party continued to thud two floors below. The smell of burnt hair was still strong. Bo sat at Cyndy's dressing table wearing Mr. Randall's bathrobe and watching herself over the perfume bottles. The mirror was rimmed with matchbooks from what looked like expensive places, a couple of dried corsages tucked between them.

"Would you like something to hug?" Cyndy asked. Bo nodded dumbly. Keeping one hand on the ice pack, Cyndy reached over to her bed and brought back a white plush polar bear. Bo took it and held it to her chest with both arms. Sometimes the nicer people were to her the worse she felt.

Cyndy took the ice pack off and inspected Bo's neck and shoulders. "It's pretty superficial, I think. The dress is finished, though, I'm afraid. Of course you could make something else out of it. There's yards and yards."

"I'm really sorry about it all, Cyndy," Bo said. "I feel like an awful fool. Maybe I was trying to start a new fashion—the towering-inferno look?"

"Cut it out. It was an accident. Could have happened to anybody." Bo definitely didn't believe that. "Listen, it could have been a lot worse."

"I could have burned the house down."

"Well, it would have been my fault," Cyndy said generously. "Me and those dumb candles. I guess I went overboard a little. But I love the effect at a party, don't you?—dumb question, Cynthia!" Cyndy said, knocking at her head and grinning. Bo sighed and wished Cyndy weren't so likable. "Hey," Cyndy said suddenly, "your parents wouldn't sue my parents, would they? I mean could they?"

"They're not the type," Bo said. Cyndy looked relieved.

"Howie's sleeping it off in Daddy's study, by the way. I had Larry and Chris move him."

"What will your folks do?" Bo asked, in spite of herself. She had pledged not to care.

"They won't be home till Monday. Anyway, even if they were here, Daddy understands these things. And don't worry, nobody else knows. There was such pandemonium down there when you lit up, nobody even noticed Howard wasn't there for you." Bo's grip tightened on the polar bear. "Poor How, he never could drink." Cyndy gave her a you-know-how-he-is look that made Bo miserable and reached for the clips that were holding up the damaged hair. "Now the question is," she said as she withdrew them, "what do we do with this?" The burnt wreckage of her best feature fell to Bo's shoulders and the smell of singed hair got worse. "Maybe I should just slice off the worst of it and you can let a pro have at it on Saturday," Cyndy said, looking at her kindly.

"Fine," Bo said softly. Cyndy opened a drawer and pulled out a leather case which read, First Award, Singer Junior Dressmaking Contest. She opened it and extracted the largest of three pairs of scissors.

•   •   •

"He called," Reenie said, meeting Bo at the door. "Four times." Bo said nothing and took off her hat. "Wow, do you look different," Reenie said and stared.

"What did you tell him?" Bo asked.

"That you weren't home. You weren't."

"Good," Bo said. "If he calls again, I'm still not."

"I'm supposed to tell a lie?" Reenie asked, horrified.

"You'll get the hang of it," Bo said and went into the kitchen.

A little while later she heard the doorbell. "I am not here," she said out loud to herself. "I am visiting another planet. Indefinitely." But whoever was at the door, it wasn't Howard. After a few minutes the kitchen door swung open and Reenie stood there clumsily holding a long white box. "He said this was for you."

"Who did?" Bo asked, feeling furious.

"The man who brought it." Bo opened the box, feeling like somebody on television. There were red roses, six of them, with some sprays of fine airy fern and a card on top of them.

"Was I supposed to give the man a tip?" Reenie said. Bo looked up blankly. "He just stood there after I took it, like he was waiting for something. I didn't have any money. What was I supposed to do?"

Bo gave the flowers a grim look. "Sell your soul," she said in reply and in a motion had gathered up the roses and the tissue and the card without even looking at it and dumped them in the kitchen trash.

The phone rang. Bo motioned to Reenie to answer it and only took the receiver from her when she was sure it wasn't Howard.

"Did you get it done?" Weezie's voice asked.

"The deed is done," Bo proclaimed lugubriously, imitating Lady Macbeth. "I feel about ten pounds lighter. Who would have thought the old girl had so much hair on her?"

"My, aren't we literary," Weezie said.

"We are indeed. In fact, I called Ms. Albersham at home this morning and told her I'd definitely be editor of *The Vigil*."

"You called her at home on a Saturday? During vacation?" Weezie exclaimed.

"She's a friend of mine. She gave me her number, didn't she? Anyway, I didn't want to change my mind so I made the commitment."

"Great," Weezie said, and got to the point. "Have you talked to Howard?"

"Did I say ten pounds lighter?" Bo said. "I meant two hundred and ten."

153

"Then you're definitely breaking it off."

"You mind telling me, friend, what exactly you mean by 'it'?" Bo asked.

"Your relationship, bimbo," Weezie said.

Bo suddenly saw herself hiding in the bathroom stall last September, and Cyndy's voice came back to her, echoing around the tile: "One person needs the other even if he won't say so. Right? A whole relationship can't just vanish."

"Wrong," Bo said aloud into the telephone.

"What?" Weezie said.

"It was wrong from the beginning. It was—one of your favorite words—pathological. Worthy of *Grotesque Romances* magazine . . ."

"Wait a minute," Weezie interrupted. "Romance implies it wasn't platonic."

"I don't know what it was, but whatever it was it's not anymore."

"Just like that?" Weezie said. "Just because he got drunk?"

"No, not *just*. And what do you mean, *just*? He just got drunk, he just abandoned me, he just made a fool of me, he just turned out to be everything I thought he wasn't," Bo said. She wanted to go on, but she couldn't think of any more grievances for the moment.

Weezie was quiet briefly and finally said, "Well, as my uncle Dewey says, 'Things aren't what they used to be—and what's more they never were.' "

"Are you saying I told you so?" Bo was getting madder. It felt good.

"Not exactly . . ." Weezie started. "I mean—"

"Good," Bo said over her. "Because believe me the experience has not been a total loss. I have learned a great deal. Actually, it's been rather cleansing."

"Do you have to throw Howard out with the bathwater?" Weezie asked.

"Why shouldn't I?" Bo practically yelled. "What good is he? I'm sorry if it bothers you and the whole of Parkview that the blubber couple will no longer be available for public appearances. I know everyone had a lot of good laughs over us, but you'll just have to seek your amusement elsewhere." Bo felt a twinge of unfairness letting that out, but it didn't stop her.

Weezie's voice was smaller than usual. "I never laughed," she said. "Did I? Did I laugh, ever?"

Bo couldn't help herself. Her anger was coming out like musket shots aimed at whoever was in the way. "You don't laugh, dear. You sneer."

"I never sneered, either," Weezie said. "I just . . . missed you."

There was a silence on the line and Weezie wondered if they'd been disconnected. "Thank you," Bo said finally, the anger gone for the moment. ". . . So, what are you doing tonight? Do you want to go to a movie or something?"

"Well, actually, I'm going out," Weezie replied, and her voice sounded funny to Bo.

"Out?" Bo said. "Who with? I mean, with whom?"

"You know him," Weezie allowed. "He's in your writing class. David Abraham?"

Bo almost choked. "I love it," she finally got out. "My baby-friend, dating boys—and if you tell me it's not a date I'll choke you over the phone. Oh, it's wonderful. You two will make beautiful music together. Beautiful snarly negative music . . . I love it . . ." She could barely contain herself.

On the other end of the line Weezie said stiffly, "It's not that funny."

"No, of course not, it's nice," Bo said. "He's nice, in a weird way. At least he doesn't misrepresent himself. Have fun," she added and got off the phone as fast as she could because she couldn't seem to stop laughing. Finally the laughter turned into choking sobs. There was no one to hold her, but she figured she'd survive.

23

In a dream that night Bo was swimming in icy, dirty water. Her hair was in her eyes. Her paws flailed around in the water. In the dream she was a polar bear. If, she thought, swimming futilely, I'm a polar bear, why am I so cold? "BUTTERRR, COME AND GET IT!" Her sister's voice. She looked up. There, on the other side of the bars watching her, were her whole family plus Howard and Weezie and Ms. Albersham and some other people she didn't know. The next minute they'd all turned into frogs. A line of frogs, watching her.

"CHOW TIME!" The voice sounded like Howard's, but she couldn't tell because everybody was a frog. She couldn't tell who was who. "CHOW TIME!" And they started throwing food at her—Raisinets, peanuts, Fritos, Oreos, and here and there a scone with butter. The food hit the rocks near her and scattered, but she couldn't reach it. She tried to climb up the sides of the pool but kept sliding down and the food kept hitting the rocks and the ground with little tapping slithery sounds, over and over . . .

156

Bo opened her eyes. The odd little tapping sounds went on, as if something were hitting somewhere and sliding. She knew now they were real. Branches scraping? Nothing grew up that high. Hail or sleet? The night was bright, following a freezing rain. So clear she could see a quarter moon out of the top of the window. She burrowed down under the covers. The sound was still there and it seemed to want her. Finally she got up and looked and saw what in her heart she expected to see: Howard Nevelson standing in her backyard, bending down getting another handful of crunchy frozen snow to throw.

She raised the window, fiddled with the storm sash, and pulled it up. It wouldn't catch. She leaned out, holding the storm sash up with her shoulder. "What are you doing?" she called in a stage whisper.

"I want to talk to you."

"No," she said.

He bent over to make another snowball. "I'll wake up everybody if I have to."

"Okay," she said furiously. "Back door." She let the window down and went to get a robe.

"I like your hair," was the first thing he said when she opened the door. She scowled and let him in. "You look different," he said, following her into the kitchen.

"So I'm told," she said.

"Are you?" She looked as though she didn't hear him. "Different?" he added.

She couldn't bear the look in his eyes. It reminded her of a sick dog. Not a sweet sick little puppy, sniffling and cuddly, but a large mixed breed, homeless and hungry and unlovable and too big to pick up. He didn't even look ashamed of himself. Just sad.

"I'm not any different," she said, knowing it was a lie. "Just smarter. I learned some things."

"Such as?" he said.

"Such as, when you think you know who people are, sometimes they're not."

"Or maybe they're more so," he added. She said nothing. He sat down. "You know," he said after a minute, "the thing I always thought was terrific about you was the way you gave everybody a break. Everybody had reasons for all the rotten things they did."

Her back was to him. She walked over to the refrigerator, opened it, surveyed its contents, and slammed it shut again.

"Okay. Is that what you came to tell me?" she said. "Reasons?" There was a threatening tone in her voice. "Go ahead. Start for example with why you had so much to drink at gorgeous Cynthia's glorious party. I mean, right from the beginning you were swilling it down!"

"Okay . . ." he started slowly. "Okay. In the first place, Cyndy gave me the first one . . ."

"So!" she jumped on him. "So of course you were forced to chugalug. And compelled to stay with your head stuck in the punch bowl. And I *do* know why. Of course I know. There you are with Lady Gargantua on your arm—the best you can do for a date under the circumstances . . ." He looked as if she'd punched him but she went on. "And there you are on your old territory, just dying to dump me, which you had to get drunk to do. It was Cyndy, wasn't it? And just being there. That's why!" Bo's eyes shone with anger and satisfaction.

"Listen," Howard said. "You asked me a question. Are you going to keep answering it yourself or what?"

"Go ahead," she said, and sat down in the chair opposite him.

"No," he replied. "Not with you sitting there looking like you're helping out on Judgment Day."

"Why did you come here, Howard?"

158

He thought a minute. "To tell you I'm sorry."

"Thank you," Bo said, not looking at his face. The refrigerator motor went on. "Now please go."

"What do you want from me?" It was as open and hurting a question as Bo had ever heard and she flinched at the sound of it. She even tried to muster the old compassion. Where was it? Had it gone up in flames with her hair that night or had it never been real, anyway? Bo didn't know and she didn't care. She couldn't help it. She just felt mean.

She finally said, "Funny you should ask that question, Howard, because that's what I've been asking me about you all this time. What does he want with me? Why, for example, did you ask me to that party? Why did you call me up long-distance and ask me to Cynthia Randall's New Year's Eve party?"

"Who else would I have asked?" He looked honestly puzzled.

"See!" Bo almost yelled in pain. "Why don't we stop this before anything worse gets said?"

"I mean it," Howard said. "I don't get you. We've been going out together for what, three months?"

"We weren't dating!" Bo raised her voice again.

"It was you who kept saying that. You who made it a big deal. I figured you were scared. I thought, okay, I like this girl. I think she's terrific. She's maybe a little weird about sex, she's maybe self-conscious because of . . . one thing and another," he finished carefully.

"Because she's fat," she corrected him.

"Whatever." He shrugged.

"And you weren't?" Bo said accusingly.

"Weren't fat? Of course I am."

"Weren't self-conscious. Weren't aware of what we looked like, what people would say. You were just Mister Magnificently Adjusted, waiting for fat little me to grow up?"

"Okay, I wasn't," Howard admitted. "I guess I wasn't any more anxious to be called the blubber couple than you were. Then after a while I wouldn't have cared, but *you* kept making a thing of it. Yeah, you did. And you made it clear you didn't want me to come near you."

"*I* did!" Bo was flabbergasted.

"You did. And what the hell, I didn't blame you."

"I don't get it," Bo said. "I don't get you. You were the one that night . . . in the snow . . . you could've and you didn't . . ."

"I wanted to," Howard said. "Believe me, but I couldn't read you. I didn't know what you wanted. I thought maybe you were teasing."

"Teasing! Me? About a thing like that?" Bo was thunderstruck.

"Or maybe," he went on, "maybe I just thought you thought I was sort of . . . safe this way . . . this size . . . and maybe that's the way you wanted it."

"Look," she said, "I don't know what I said to . . ." She stopped because Howard wasn't listening.

"So Cyndy calls me at Marcia's place a couple of weeks later," he went on, "and she says party and I think, why not? It's a civilized world. We've got new interests now. Even if the interest isn't interested." He paused to let that sink in. "And it's not like she and I'd been engaged."

"You were pretty hot stuff, I heard. Last year."

"Last year," Howard said, and looked her straight in the eye, "is beside the point. Only it isn't for you, is it? You're still living there. That's what I didn't figure out. That's where I went wrong." He looked at her furiously. Bo was reeling.

"Howard," she said. "Could you tell me what you mean, because I honestly don't know." She had stopped looking like a judge.

"Okay," he said, after a minute. "I was pretty big stuff to you last year, wasn't I? During the freshman show?"

Bo couldn't help the look that came into her eyes but it seemed to make things harder for him. "Yeah," he said softly, "like that. It was easy for me. Tippy calls me because I'm some kind of big-man-on-campus type, and I do my thing and everybody thinks Nevelson's God's grandson, and I won't kid you, I liked the feeling. I liked the look in your eyes over me. I liked the way a lot of people looked at me then. I ate it up!"

"That's natural," Bo said, wanting for some reason to defend him. "That's only natural."

"Thank you very much!" Howard's voice was loud and shaking. "Thank you for your profound understanding of my weaknesses!"

Bo felt frightened suddenly. "I never said you were weak! I never even thought it!"

"Exactly!" Howard said, as if she'd hit a bull's-eye. "And that's where I screwed up. Because I thought *you* were the one I didn't have to win any awards for. I figured you knew when I came back this year that I wasn't your Mr. Big after all—and that was okay with you."

"Well it was! It is!" Bo felt like she was choking.

"Don't kid yourself, *dear heart*," he said, glaring at her. "The only weaknesses you get off on are the ones you've got, too. It was fine as long as we were a matched pair. I eat too much, you eat too much, we can feel crummy about that together."

"You've got it all mixed up," Bo said. "You made me feel good about me. Not just back then, but now—this whole semester. Until the other night."

"When I fell off my white horse." Bo put her face in her hands. "You were right, you know," he said. "About being there. And Cyndy." Bo pressed her hands harder into her face. "Not because I wanted her, because I don't. See, I

161

thought I could hack it—going in there, you and me, what-ever people thought about it—but you kept sort of pulling away and being nervous and I wanted to take care of you, too, and somewhere, dammit, I wanted to be Howard Hero again. And the fact is, I couldn't handle any of it. So I got sloshed." It was quiet again. Bo peeked through her fingers. He was looking at the pattern on the linoleum, tracing it with his foot. "I hurt you, and I'm sorry," he said.

She couldn't quite give. "You disappointed me. And you embarrassed me. And you humiliated me," she said through her hands and then took them away.

"I know, Barbara. I've been trying all day to tell you I'm sorry. But that's the best I can do."

Bo sat there a minute, not knowing what to do. Finally she got up and walked across the room, pretty sure he would follow her. She turned around and said slowly, "I'm sorry, too, I guess. I'm not even sure for what. Maybe for asking too much?"

"I think it's okay to ask," he said. "Maybe you just shouldn't count on getting it."

"You counted on something from me I couldn't give you, either," she admitted. "So I guess we're about even."

"We always were," he said. "I knew that, even if you didn't, way last spring."

Bo thought about that a moment. "Maybe," she said, working it out as she spoke, "*that* is what I didn't really want to know. Not everything that meant. It was easier to think you were so much better."

"Not for me," he said simply.

"I'm sorry, Howard," she said, and this time she knew what for.

The refrigerator motor went off, and it was completely quiet in the kitchen. Finally they kissed each other. Bo had thought about it so often that it didn't feel like the first time.

"I think we should have some rules," Bo said, a few minutes later. "Or at least some guidelines."

"I wasn't expecting to rush anything," Howard said.

Bo blushed. "I wasn't talking about that sort of thing," she said. "Let's say . . . I will expect you to be maybe only ninety percent wonderful."

"Could you go for seventy-five?" Howard asked, and touched her hair.

"Seventy-five it is," Bo said. "And I will make every attempt not to fix the remaining twenty-five."

"Who asked you?" Howard wondered.

"Exactly," Bo said.

He touched her hair again. "I like it short," he said. "I can see more of you."

"There's lots to see, heaven knows. I may even get around to doing something about that soon."

"Fine with me," he said generously.

"Thanks a heap," she said, and added, "And you may or may not come along."

"I'll think about it," he said and kissed her again.

"Incidentally," she said after a moment, "thank you for the flowers. I'm sorry I didn't appreciate them at the time."

"Flowers?" Howard said, looking blank. A startled Bo dived for the kitchen trash. The limp roses were still on top. She scratched her hand fumbling for the card. When she finally found it and read it, she put one hand over her mouth and handed the card to Howie. It read, "To a flaming beauty. Kindest regards, Dodson L. White."

"That son of a gun," Howard sputtered. "What does he want, a punch in the nose?"

Bo laughed and went to get a vase.

"You can't put those out," he said, following her. "They're all droopy."

"As a friend of mine is fond of saying"—Bo grinned as

she stuck the flowers in water—''I guess ya works with what ya got.''

She set the roses in the middle of the kitchen table. They slumped a little but looked as though they could sing.

About the Author

JUDITH PINSKER was born and grew up in western New York. She has worked as a television scriptwriter, a publicist, a symphony manager, and a secretary. She now lives in St. Louis, Missouri, with her husband and son. This is her first novel.

Romance Has Never Been So Much Fun!

☐ **LOVE AT THE LAUNDROMAT**
by Rona S. Zable   **27225-X $2.95**
Sixteen-year-old Jo can't believe her mother has invested
their life savings in a laundromat! Does she really think
she can turn the coin-op into a successful financial
investment *and* a cultural center? But everyone does
have dirty laundry, including handsome college guys
like Scott Ashley! Is it possible to sort out romance
with the laundry?

☐ **CAMP GIRL-MEETS-BOY**
by Caroline B. Cooney   **27273-X $2.95**
Welcome to Camp Menunkechogue! For Marissa, finally
a counselor, camp is what she lives for. For Vi, camp
is a place to meet and catch a boyfriend. Grab your gear
and join them for camp songs, romance, and great
summer friendships!

Watch for CAMP REUNION, coming in October!

Bantam Books, Dept. DA25, 414 East Golf Road,
Des Plaines, IL 60016

Please send me the books I have checked above. I am enclosing
$_____ (please add $2.00 to cover postage and handling).
Send check or money order—no cash or C.O.D.s please.

Mr/Ms _____

Address _____

City/State _____ Zip _____
                                            DA25—3/89
Please allow four to six weeks for delivery. This offer expires 9/89.
Prices and availability subject to change without notice.